OLIVI

BY

O. DOUGLAS

AUTHOR OF "THE SETONS" "PENNY PLAIN" ETC

HODDER AND STOUGHTON
LIMITED   LONDON

First Edition printed November 1912
Second Edition . . April 1913
Third Edition . . April 1918
Fourth Edition . . January 1922
and this the Fifth Edition, March 1922

PRINTED IN GREAT BRITAIN BY MORRISON AND GIBB LTD., EDINBURGH

CONTENTS

PART I

PART II

PART III

PART IV

THROUGH THE GATES OF THE EAST

S.S. Scotia, Oct. 19, 19—.

. . . THIS is a line to send off with the pilot. There is nothing to say except " Good-bye " again.

We have had luncheon, and I have been poking things out of my cabin trunk, and furtively surveying one—there are two, but the other seems to be lost at present—of my cabin companions. She has fair hair and a blue motor-veil, and looks quiet and subdued, but then, I dare say, so do I.

I hope you are thinking of your friend going down to the sea in a ship.

I feel, somehow, very small and lonely.

OLIVIA.

S.S Scotia, Oct. 21.

(In pencil.)

. . . WHATEVER you do, whatever folly you commit, never, never be tempted to take a sea voyage. It is quite the nastiest thing you can take —I have had three days of it now, so I know.

When I wrote to you on Saturday I had an uneasy feeling that in the near future all would not be well with me, but I went in to dinner and afterwards walked up and down the deck trying to feel brave. Sunday morning dawned rain-washed and tempestuous, and the way the ship heaved was not encouraging, but I rose, or rather I descended from my perch—did I tell you I had an upper berth ?—and walked with an undulating motion towards my bath. Some people would have remained in bed, or at least gone unbathed, but, as I say, I rose—mark, please, the rugged grandeur of the Scots character—and such is the force of example the fair-haired girl rose also. Before I go any further I must tell you about this girl. Her name is Hilton, Geraldine Hilton, but as that is too long a name and already we are great friends, I call her G. She is very pretty, with the kind of prettiness that becomes more so the more you look—and if you don't know what I mean I can't stop to explain —with masses of yellow hair, such blue eyes and pink cheeks and white teeth that I am convinced I am sharing a cabin with the original Hans Andersen's Snow Queen. She is very big and most healthy, and delightful to look at ; even sea-sickness does not make her look plain, and that, you will admit, is a severe test; and what is more, her nature is as healthy and sweet as her face. You will laugh and say it is like me to know all about anyone in three days, but two sea-sick and home-sick people shut up in a tiny cabin can exhibit quite a lot of traits, pleasant and otherwise, in three days

Well, we dressed, and reaching the saloon, sank into our seats only to leave again hurriedly when a steward approached to know if we would have porridge or kippered herring ! I know you are never sea-sick, unlovable creature that you are, so you won't sympathize with us as we lay limp and wretched in our deck-chairs on the damp and draughty deck. Even the fact that our deck-chairs were brand-new, and had our names boldly painted in handsome black letters across the back, failed to give us a thrill of pleasure. At last it became too utterly miserable to be borne. The sight of the deck-steward bringing round cups of half-cold beef-tea with grease spots floating on the top proved the last straw, so, with a graceful, wavering flight like a woodcock, we zigzagged to our bunks, where we have remained ever since.

I don't know where we are. I expect Ushant

has slammed the door on us long ago   Our little
world is bounded by the four walls of the cabin.
All day we lie and listen to the swish of the waves
as they tumble past, and watch our dressing-gowns
hanging on the door swing backwards and forwards
with the motion   At intervals the stewardess comes
in, a nice Scotswoman,—Corrie, she tells me, is
her home-place,—and brings the menu of breakfast
—luncheon—dinner, and we turn away our heads
and say, " Nothing—nothing ! "   Our steward is a
funny little man, very small and thin, with pale
yellow hair ; he reminds me of a moulting canary,
and his voice cheeps and is rather canary-like too.
He is really a very kind little steward and trots
about most diligently on our errands, and tries to
cheer us by tales of the people he has known who
have died of sea-sickness : " Strained their 'earts,
Miss, that's wot they done ! "   It isn't very cheerful
lying here, looking out through the port-hole, now
at the sky, next at the sea, but what it would
have been without G. I dare not think   We have
certainly helped each other through this time
of trial   It is a wonderful blessing, a companion
in misfortune.

But where, you may ask, is the third occupant
of the cabin ?   Would it not have been fearful if

she, too, had been stretched on a couch of languish-
ing ? Happily she is a good sailor, though she
'doesn't look it. She is a little woman with a pale
green complexion and a lot of sleek black hair,
and somehow gives one the impression of having a
great many more teeth than is usual. Her name
is Mrs. Murray, and she is going to India to rejoin
her husband, who rejoices in the name of Albert.
Sometimes I feel a little sorry for Albert, but perhaps, after all, he deserves what he has got. She
has very assertive manners   I think she regards G.
and me as two young women who want keeping in
their places, though I am sure we are humble
enough now whatever we may be in a state of rude
health   Happily she has friends on board, so she
rarely comes to the cabin except to tidy up before
meals, and afterwards to tell us exactly everything
she has eaten   She seems to have a good appetite
and to choose the things that sound nastiest when
one is seedy

No—I don't like Mrs. Murray much ; but I dislike her hat-box more. It is large and square and
black, and it has no business in the cabin, it ought
to be in the baggage-room   Lying up here I am
freed from its tyranny, but on Saturday, when I
was unpacking, it made my life a burden. It

blocks up the floor under my hooks, and when I hang things up I fall over it backwards, when I sit on the floor, which I have to do every time I pull out my trunk, it hits me savagely on the spine, and once, when I tried balancing it on a small chest of drawers, it promptly fell down on my head and I have still a large and painful bump as a memento.

I wonder if you will be able to make this letter out? I am writing it a little bit at a time, to keep myself from getting too dreadfully down-hearted. G. and I have both very damp handkerchiefs under our pillows to testify to the depressed state of our minds. "When I was at home I was in a better place, but travellers must be content."

I don't even care to read any of the books I brought with me, except now and then a page or two of *Memories and Portraits*. It comforts me to read of such steady, quiet places as the Pentland Hills and of the decent men who do their herding there.

Is it really only three days since I left you all, and you envied me going out into the sunshine? Oh! you warm, comfortable people, how I, in this heaving uncertain horror of a ship, envy you!

25th.

(Still in pencil.)

You mustn't think I have been lying here all the time. On Tuesday we managed to get on deck, and on Wednesday it was warm and sunny, and we began to enjoy life again and to congratulate ourselves on having got our sea-legs. But we got them only to lose them, for yesterday the wind got up, the ship rolled, we became every minute more thoughtful, until about tea-time we retired in disorder. It didn't need the little steward's shocked remark, " Oh my ! You never 'ave gone back to bed again ! " to make us feel ashamed.

However, we reach Marseilles to-day at noon, and, glorious thought, the ship will stand still for twenty-four hours. Also there will be letters !

This isn't a letter so much as a wail.

Don't scoff. I know I'm a coward.

S S. Scotia, Oct. 27.

. . . A FOUNTAIN-PEN is really a great comfort I am writing with my new one, so this letter won't, I hope, be such a puzzle to decipher as my pencil scrawl.

We are off again, but now the sun shines from a cloudless sky on a sea of sapphire, and the passengers are sunning themselves on deck like snails after a shower. I'm glad, after all, I didn't go back from Marseilles by train.

When we reached Marseilles the rain was pouring, but that didn't prevent us ("us" means G. and myself) from bounding on shore. We found a dilapidated *fiacre* driven by a still more dilapidated *cocher*, who, for the sum of six francs, drove us to the town. I don't know whether, ordinarily, Marseilles is a beautiful town or an ugly one. Few people, I expect, would have seen anything attractive in it this dark, rainy October afternoon, but to us it was a sort of Paradise regained. We had tea at a café, real French tea tasting of hay-seed and lukewarm water, and real French cakes; we wandered through the streets, stopping to stare in at every shop window; we bought violets to adorn ourselves, and picture-postcards, and sheets of foreign stamps for Peter, and all the time the rain poured and the street lamps were cheerily reflected in the wet pavements, and it was so damp, and dark, and dirty, and home-like, we sloppered joyfully through the mud and were happy for the first time for a whole week. The thought of letters was the only thing that tempted us back to the ship.

I heard from all the home people,—even Peter wrote, a most characteristic epistle with only about half the words wrongly spelt, and finishing with a spirited drawing of the *Scotia* attacked by pirates, an abject figure crouching in the bows being labelled " You ! " How I miss that young brother of mine ! I ache to see his nubbly features (" nubbly " is a portmanteau word and exactly describes them) and the hair that no brush can persuade to lie straight, and to hear the broad accent—a legacy from a nurse who hailed from a mining village in Lithgow—which is such a trial to his relatives I have no illusions about Peter's looks any more than he has himself A too candid relative commenting once on his excessive plainness in his presence, he replied, " Yes, I know, but I've a nice good face. " I sometimes feel that if Peter turns out badly it will be greatly my fault. Mother was so busy with many things that I naturally, as the big sister, did most of the training, and it wasn't easy When I read to him on Sunday *Tales of the Covenanters*, he at once made up his mind that he much preferred Claverhouse to John Brown of Priesthill, an unheard-of heresy, and yawning vigorously, announced that he was as dull as a bull and as sick as a daisy. One night when I went to hear him say his prayers, he said :

"I'm not going to say any prayers."

"Oh, Peter," I said, "why?"

"'Cos I've prayed for a whole year it would be snow on Christmas and it wasn't—just rain."

"Then," I said very gravely, "God won't take care of you through the night."

"Put me in my bed," said the little ruffian, "and I'll see;" and I was awakened at break of day by a small figure in pyjamas dancing at my bedside, shouting with unholy joy, "I'm here, you see, I'm here," and it was weeks before I could bring him to a better state of mind.

So much younger than any of us—the other boys were at Oxford when he was in his first knicker-bockers—he was a lonely little soul and lived in a world of his own, peopled by the creatures of his own imaginings His great friend was Mr. Bath-both of Bathboth—don't you like the name?—and he would come in from a walk with his nurse, fling down his cap and remark, "I've been seeing Mr. Bathboth in his own house—oh! a lovely house. It's a *public-house*!"

I'm afraid he was a very low character this

Mr. Bathboth. According to Peter, "he smoked, and he swored, and he put his fingers to his nose when his mother said he wasn't to," so we weren't surprised to hear of his end. He was pulled up to heaven by a crane for bathing in the sea on Sunday. Another of Peter's creatures was a bogle called "Windy Wallops" who lived in the garrets and could only be repulsed with hairbrushes "Whippetie Stoowrie," on the other hand, was a kindly creature inhabiting the nursery chimney, and given to laying small offerings such as a pistol and caps or a sugar mouse on the fender. A strange fancy once took Peter to dig graves for us all in the garden. It wasn't that he disliked us ; on the contrary, he considered he was doing us an honour. My grave was suggestively near the rubbish-heap, but he pointed out that it was because the lily-of-the-valley grew there. One day he came in earthy but determined-looking. "Dodo didn't send me anything for my birthday," he announced, "so I've *filled up his grave.*"

Now Peter has gone to school and has put away childish things, and the desire to be a knight like Launcelot. He no longer babbles to himself in such a way as to make strangers doubt of his sanity ; and he confided to me lately that when he grew

up he hoped to lead a Double Life. He who was
brought up in Camelot, he who wept when Roland
at Roncesvalles blew his horn for the last time, now
devours blood-curdling detective stories, vile things
in paper covers, which he keeps concealed about his
person, and whips out at odd moments. What he
hates is a book with the slightest hint of a love
affair. I found him disgustedly punching a book
with his fist and muttering (evidently to the hero),
" I know you, I know you, you're in love with her,"
in tones of bitter scorn. When I begin to speak
about Peter I can't stop, and forget how tiresome
it must be for people to listen. I apologize, but
please bear with me when I enlarge upon this
brother of mine ; I simply must, sometimes.

How good of you to write such a long letter !
Of course I shall write often and at length, but
you must promise not to be bored, or expect too
much. I fear you won't get anything very wise
or witty from me. You know how limited I am.
The fairies, when they came to my christening,
might have come better provided with gifts. But
then, I expect they have only a certain number
of gifts for each family, so I don't in the least blame
them for giving the boys the brains and giving me—
what ? At the moment I can't think of anything

they did give me except a heart that keeps on the
windy side of care, as Beatrice puts it ; and hair
that curls naturally.   I have no grudge against the
fairies.   If they had given me straight hair and
brains I might have been a Suffragist and shamed
my kin by biting a policeman , and *that* would
have been a pity.

Later.

G. and I are crouched in a corner, very awed and
sad. A poor man died suddenly yesterday from
heart failure, and the funeral is just over.   I do hope
I shall never again see a burial at sea.   It was
terrible.   The bell tolled and the ship slowed down
and almost stopped, while the body, wrapped in a
Union Jack, was slipped into the water, committed
to the deep in sure and certain hope of a blessed
resurrection   In a minute it was all over.

The people are laughing and talking again ;
the dressing-bugle has sounded ; things go on as if
nothing had happened. We are steaming ahead,
leaving the body—such a little speck it looked on
the great water—far behind

It is the utter loneliness of it that makes me
cry !

S.S Scotia, Oct. 29.

. . . THIS won't be a tidy letter, for I am sitting close beside the rail—has it a nautical name? I don't know—and every few minutes the spray comes over and wets the paper and incidentally myself. *And* the fountain-pen! I greatly fear it leaks, for my middle finger is blackened beyond hope of cleansing, and though not ten minutes ago Mr. Brand inked himself very comprehensively filling it for me, already it requires frequent shakings to make it write at all. I thought it would be a blessing, it threatens to become a curse. I foresee that very shortly I shall descend again to a pencil, or write my letters with the aid of scratchy pens and fat, respectable ink-pots in the stuffy music-room.

You will have two letters from Port Said. The one I wrote you two days ago finished in deep melancholy, but to-day it is so good to be alive I could shout with joy. I woke this morning with a jump of delight, and even Mrs. Albert Murray—she of the hat-box and the many teeth—could not irritate me, and you can't think how many irritating ways the woman has It is 10 a.m. and we have just come up from breakfast, and have got our deck-chairs placed where they will catch every breeze (and some salt water), and, with a pile of books and two boxes of chocolate, are comfortably settled for the day.

You ask about the passengers.

We have all sorts and conditions. Quiet people who read and work all day; rowdy people who never seem happy unless they are throwing cushions or pulling one another downstairs by the feet; painfully enterprising people who get up sports, sweeps, concerts, and dances, and are full of a tiresome, misplaced energy; bridge-loving people who play from morning till night; flirtatious people who frequent dark corners; happy people who laugh; sad people who sniff; and one man who can't be classed with anyone else, a sad gentleman, his hair standing fiercely on end, a Greek Testament his constant and only companion. We pine to know who and what he is and where he is going. Yesterday I found myself beside him at tea. I might not have existed for all the notice he took of me. "Speak to him," said G. in my ear. "You don't dare!"

Of course after that I had to, so pinching G.'s arm to give myself courage, I said in a small voice, "Are you enjoying the voyage?"

He turned, regarded me with his sad prominent
eyes. "Do I look as if I enjoyed it?" asked
this Monsieur Melancholy, and went back to his
bread-and-butter.   G. choked, and I finished my
tea hurriedly and in silence

Nearly everyone on board seems nice and willing
to be pleasant. I am on smiling terms with most
and speaking terms with many, but one really sees
very little of the people outside one's own little set.
It is odd how people drift together and make cliques.
There are eight in our particular set.   Colonel and
Mrs. Crawley, Major and Mrs. Wilmot; Captain
Gordon, Mr. Brand, G., and myself.   The Crawleys,
the Wilmots, and Captain Gordon are going back
after furlough; Mr. Brand and G. and I are going
only for pleasure and the cold weather. Our
table is much the merriest in the saloon. Mrs.
Crawley is a fascinating woman; I never tire
watching her. Very pretty, very smart with a
pretty wit, she has the most delightfully gay,
infectious laugh, which contrasts oddly with her
curiously sad, unsmiling eyes. Mrs. Wilmot has a
Madonna face. I don't mean one of those silly,
fat-faced Madonnas one sees in the Louvre and elsewhere, but one's own idea of the Madonna; the
kind of face, as someone puts it, that God must love.

She isn't pretty and she isn't in the least smart,
but she is just a kind, sweet, wise woman. Her
husband is a cheery soul, very big and boyish and
always in uproarious spirits. Captain Gordon
makes a good listener. Mr. Brand, although he
must have left school quite ten years ago, is still
very reminiscent of Eton and has a school-boyish
taste in silly rhymes and riddles. Colonel Crawley,
a stern and somewhat awe-inspiring man, a dis-
tinguished soldier, I am told, hates *passionately*
being asked riddles, and we make him frantic
at table repeating Mr. Brand's witticisms. He sits
with a patient, disgusted face while we repeat,

> " Owen More had run away
> Owin' more than he could pay ;
> Owen More came back one day
> Owin' more " ;

and when he can bear it no longer leaves the table
remarking *Titbits*. He had his revenge the other
day, when the ship was rolling more than a little.
We had ventured to the saloon for tea and were
surveying uncertainly some dry toast, when Colonel
Crawley came in. "Ah!" he said, "Steward!
Pork chops for these ladies." The mere thought
proved the thing too much, we fled to the fresh air
—tealess.

I meant this to be a very long letter, but this pen,
aint yet pursuing, shows signs of giving out.   I
ıave to shake it every second word now.

The bugle has gone for lunch, and G., who has
ıeen sound asleep for the last hour, is uncoiling her-
;elf preparatory to going down.

So good-bye.

S S. Scotia, Nov. 1.

. . . ALL day we have glided through the Canal.
Imagine a shining band of silver water, a band of
leepest blue sky, and in between a bar of fine gold
which is the desert—and you have some idea of
what I am looking at.   Sometimes an Arab passes
riding on a camel, and I can't get away from the
feeling that I am a child again looking at a highly
:oloured Bible picture-book on Sabbath afternoons.

We landed at Port Said yesterday morning.
People told us it was a dirty place, an uninteresting
place, a horribly dull place, not worth leaving the
ship to see, but it was our first glimpse of the East
ınd we were enchanted.   The narrow streets, the
white domes and minarets against the blue sky,

the flat roofs of the houses, the queer shops with the Arabs shouting to draw attention to their wares, and, above all, the new strange smell of the East, were, to us, wonderful and fascinating.

When we got ashore the sun was shining with a directness hitherto unknown to us, making the backs of our unprotected heads feel somewhat insecure, so we went first to a shop where we spied exposed to sale a rich profusion of topis. In case you don't know, a topi is a sun-hat, a white thing, large and saucer-like, lined with green, with cork about it somewhere, rather suggestive of a lifebelt; horribly unbecoming but quite necessary.

A very polite man bowed us inside, and we proceeded on our quixotic search for a topi not entirely hideous. Half an hour later we came out of the shop, the shopman more obsequious than ever, not only wearing topis, but laden with boxes of Turkish Delight, ostrich-feather fans, tinsel scarves, and a string of pink beads which he swore were coral, but I greatly doubt it. We had an uneasy feeling as we bought the things that perhaps we were foolish virgins, but before the afternoon was very old we were sure of it. You wouldn't believe how heavy Turkish Delight becomes when you carry half a dozen boxes for some hours under a blazing sun, and I had a carved book-rest under one arm, and G. had four parcels and a green umbrella. To complete our disgust, after weltering under our purchases for some time we saw in a shop exactly the same things much cheaper. G. pointed a wrathful finger, letting two parcels fall to do it. "Look at that," she said. "I'm going straight back to tell the man he's cheated us." With difficulty I persuaded her it wasn't worth while, and tired and dusty we sank—no, we didn't sink, they were iron chairs —we sat down hard on chairs outside a big hotel and demanded tea immediately. Some of the ship people were also having tea at little tables, and a party of evil-looking Frenchmen were twanging guitars and singing sentimental songs for pennies. While we were waiting a man—an Arab, I think— crouched beside us and begged us to let him read our hands for half a crown, and we were weak enough to permit it. You may be interested to know that I am to be married "soon already" to a high official with gold in his teeth. It sounds ideal. G. was rather awed by the varied career he sketched for her. After tea, which was long in coming and when it came disappointing, we had still some time, so we hailed a man driving a depressed-looking horse attached to a carriage of sorts,

and told him to drive us all round   He looked a
very wicked man, but it may have been the effect of
his only having one eye, for he certainly had a refined taste in sights.   When we suggested that we
would like to see the Arab bazaar he shook his head
violently, and instead drove us along dull roads,
stopping now and again to wave a vague whip towards some building, remarking in most melancholy
tones as he did so, " The English Church "—" The
American Mission."

Back on the ship again, sitting on deck in the
soft darkness, watching the lights of the town and
hearing a faint echo of the life there, I realized with
something of a shock that it was Hallow-e'en.
Does that convey nothing to your mind ?   To me
it brings back memories of cold, fast-shortening
days, and myself jumping long-legged over cabbage-
stalks in the kitchen-garden, chanting—

> " This is the nicht o' Hallow-e'en
> When a' the witches will be seen—"

in fearful hope of seeing a witch, not mounted on a
broomstick, but on the respectable household cat,
changed for that night into a flying fury ; finally,
along with my brothers, being captured, washed,
and dressed, to join with other spirits worse than
ourselves in " dooking " for apples and eating

mashed potatoes in momentary expectation of
swallowing a threepenny-bit or a thimble   To-
night, far from the other spirits, far from the chili
winds and the cabbage-stalks, I have been watching
the sunset on the desert making the world a glory
of rose and gold and amethyst.   Now it is dark , the
lights are lit all over the ship ; the floor of heaven
is thick inlaid with patines of bright gold . . .

> " In such a night did young Lorenzo . . ."

Nov. 2, 11.30 *a m.*

OUR fellow-passengers derive much amusement
from the way we sit and scribble, and one man
asked me if I were writing a book ! All this time
I haven't mentioned the Port Said letters. We
got them before we left the ship, and, determined
for once to show myself a well-balanced, sensible
young person, I took mine to the cabin and locked
them firmly in a trunk, telling myself how nice it
would be to read them in peace on my return
The spirit was willing, but—I found I must rush
down to take just a peep to see if everyone was
well, and the game ended with me sitting uncomfortably on the knobby edge of Mrs. Albert Murray's
bunk, breathlessly tearing open envelopes.

They were all delightful, and I have read them many times. I have yours beside me now, and to make it like a real talk I shall answer each point as it comes.

You say the sun hasn't shone since I left.

Are you by any chance paying me a compliment ? Or are you merely stating a fact ? As Pet Marjorie would say, I am primmed up with majestic pride because of the compliments I receive. One lady, whose baby I held for a little this morning, told me I had such a sweet, unspoiled disposition ! But what really pleased me and made me feel inches taller was that Captain Gordon told someone who told me that he thought I had great stability of character. It is odd how one loves to be told one has what one hasn't ! I, who have no more stability of character than a pussy-cat, felt ·warm with gratitude. Only—I should like to make my exit now before he discovers how mistaken he is !

Yes, I wish you were sitting by my side racing through the waves. Indeed, I wish all my dear people were here.

Are you really feeling lonely, you popular young man of many engagements ? " Lonely and dissatisfied " are your words. But why ? Why ? Surely no one ever had less reason to feel dissatis-

fied. There are very many people, my friend, who
wouldn't mind being you. And yet you aren't
thankful! Not thankful for the interesting life
you have, the plays you see, the dinners you eat,
the charming women you talk to, the balls you
dance at, the clubs you frequent—though what a
man does at his clubs beyond escaping for a brief
season from his womenkind I never quite know.
Think how nice to be a man and not have to look
pleased when one is really bored to extinction!
If you are bored you have only to slip away to
your most comfortable rooms. Did I tell you how
much I liked your rooms that day Margie and I went
to tea with you ? or were we too busy talking about
other things ? Now don't be like Peter He was
grumbling about something and I told him to go
away and count his blessings. He went obediently,
and returned triumphant. " I've done it ! " he
said, " and I've six things to be thankful for and
nine to be unthankful for——"

One thing for which I think you might feel
" unthankful " is your lamentable lack of near
relations. It is hard to be quite alone in the world ;
for, I agree, aunts don't count for much. Weighed
in the balance they are generally found woefully
wanting.

I remember once, when we were laughing over some escapade of our childhood you said you had no very pleasant recollection of your childish days, that you didn't look forward to holidays and that your happiest time was at school, because then you had companions.

I feel quite sad when I think what you missed. We were very lucky, four of us growing up together, and I sometimes wonder if other children had the same full, splendid time we had, and if they employed it getting into as many scrapes. The village people, shaking their heads over us and our probable end, used to say, " They're a' bad, but the lassie (meaning me) is the verra deil." We were bad, but we were also extraordinarily happy. I treasure up all sorts of memories, some of them very trivial and absurd, store them away in lavender, and when I feel dreary I take them out and refresh myself with them. One episode I specially remember, though why I should tell you about it I don't quite know, for it is a small thing and " silly sooth." We were staying at the time with our grandmother, the grandmother I am called for, a very stern and stately lady—the only person I have ever really stood in awe of We had been wandering all day, led by John, searching for hidden

treasure at the rainbow's foot, climbing high hills
to see if the world came to an end at the other
side, or some equally fantastic quest. It was dark
and almost supper-time and we had committed
the heinous crime of not appearing for tea, so,
when we were told to go at once to see our grandmother, and stumbled just as we were, tired and
dusty, hair on end and stockings at our ankles,
into the quiet room where she sat knitting fleecy
white things by the table with the lamp, we expected nothing better than to be sent straight to
bed, probably supperless. Our grandmother laid
down her knitting, took off her spectacles, and
instead of the rebuke we expected and deserved
said, " Bairns, come away in. I'm sure you must
be tired." It had been an unsuccessful day ; we
had found no treasure, not even the World's End ;
the night had fallen damp, with an eerily sighing
wind which depressed us vaguely as we trudged
homewards ; but now, the black night shut out,
there was the fire-light and the lamp-light, the kind
old voice, and the delicious sense of having come
home.

All things considered, you are a young man greatly
to be envied, also at the present moment to be
scolded. How can you possibly allow yourself to

think such silly things? You must have a most exaggerated idea of my charms if you think every man on board must be in love with me. Men aren't so impressionable. Did you think that when my well-nigh unearthly beauty burst on them they would fall on their knees and with one voice exclaim, " Be mine ! " I assure you no one has ever even thought of doing anything of the kind, and if they had *I wouldn't tell you*. I know you are only chaffing, but I do so hate all that sort of thing, and to hear people talk of their " conquests " is revolting. One of the nicest things about G. is that she doesn't care a bit to philander about with men. She and I are much happier talking to each other, a fact which people seem to find hard to believe.

My attention is being diverted from my writing by a lady sitting a few yards away—the Candle we call her because so many silly young moths hover round. She is a buxom person, with very golden hair growing darker towards the roots, hard blue eyes, and a powdery white face. G. and I are intensely interested to know what is the attraction about her, for no one can deny there is one. She isn't young; the gods have not made her fair, and I doubt of her honesty; yet from the first she has been surrounded by men—most of them,

I grant you, unfinished youths bound to offices in
Calcutta, but still men. I thought it might be her
brilliant conversation, but for the last half-hour
I have listened,—indeed we have no choice but to
listen, the voices are so strident,—and it can't be
that, because it isn't brilliant or even amusing,
unless to call men names like Pyjamas, or Fatty,
or Tubby, and slap them playfully at intervals
is amusing. A few minutes ago Mrs. Crawley
came to sit with us looking so fresh in a white
linen dress. I don't know why it is—she wears
the simplest clothes, and yet she manages to make
all the other women look dowdy. She has the gift,
too, of knowing the right thing to wear on every
occasion. At Port Said, for instance, the costumes
were varied The Candle flopped on shore in a
trailing white lace dress and an enormous hat ;
some broiled in serge coats and skirts ; Mrs. Crawley
in a soft green muslin and rose-wreathed hat was
a cool and dainty vision. Well, to return. As
Mrs. Crawley shook up her chintz cushions, she
looked across at the Candle—a long look that took
in the elaborate golden hair, the much too smart
blouse, the abbreviated skirt showing the high-
heeled slippers, the crowd of callow youths—and
then, smiling slightly to herself, settled down in

her chair. I grew hot all over for the Candle. I
don't suppose I need trouble myself I expect
she is used to having women look at her like that,
and doesn't mind Does she really like silly boys
so much and other women so little, I wonder!
There is generally something rather nasty about a
woman who declares she can't get on with other
women and whom other women don't like. Men
have an absurd notion that we can't admire another
woman or admit her good points. It isn't so
We admire a pretty woman just as much as you do.
The only difference is you men think that if a
woman has a lovely face it follows, as the night
the day, that she must have a lovely disposition.
We know better that's all

   The poor Candle! I feel so mean and guilty
writing about her under her very eyes, so to speak.
She looked at me just now quite kindly. I have a
good mind to tear this up, but after all what does
it matter? My silly little observations won't
make any impression on your masculine mind.
Only don't say " Spiteful little cat," because I don't
mean to be, really.

   This is much the longest letter I ever wrote.
You will have to read a page at a time and then
take a long breath and try again,

Mr. Brand has just come up to ask us why a
sculptor dies a horrible death ?   Do you know ?

                                    S.S. Scotia, Nov 6.

No one unendowed with the temper of an angel
and the ꞇpatience of a Job should attempt the
voyage to India.   Mrs. Albert Murray has neither
of these qualifications any more than I have, and
for two days she hasn't deigned to address a remark
to G. or me, all because of a lost pair of stockings ;
a loss which we treated with unseemly levity
However, the chill haughtiness of our cabin companion is something of a relief in this terrible heat.
For it *is* hot.   I am writing in the cabin, and in
spite of the fact that there are two electric fans
buzzing on either side of me, I am hotter than I
can say, and deplorably ill-tempered.   Four times
this morning, trying to keep out of Mrs. Albert
Murray's way, I have fallen over that wretched
hat-box, still here despite our hints about the
baggage-room, and now in revenge I am sitting on
it, though what the owner would say, if she came
in suddenly and found to what base uses I had put

her treasure, I dare not let myself think. G. has
a bad headache, and it is dull for her to be alone,
so that is the reason why I am in the cabin at all.
To be honest, it is most unpleasant on deck, rainy
with a damp, hot wind blowing, and the music-room
is crowded and stuffy beyond words, or I might
not be unselfish enough to remain with G. I did
go up, and a fat person, whose nurse was ill, gave
me her baby to hold, a poor white-faced, fretful
baby, who pulled down all my hair, and I have had
the unpleasant task of doing it up again. If you
have ever stood in a very hot greenhouse with the
door shut, and wrestled with something above
your head, you will know what I felt.

We passed Aden yesterday and stopped for a
few hours to coal. That was the limit. The sun
beating down on the deck, the absence of the
slightest breeze, coal-dust sifting into everything—
ouf ! Aden's barren rocks reminded me rather of
the Skye Coolin. I wonder if they are climbable.
I haven't troubled you much, have I, with accounts
of the entertainments on board ? but I think I
must tell you about a whistling competition we
had the other day. You must know that we had
each a partner, and the women sat at one end of
the deck and the men stood at the other and were

told the tune they had to whistle, when they rushed to us and each whistled his tune to his partner, who had to write the name on a piece of paper and hand it back, and the man who got back to the umpire first won—at least his partner did. Do you understand? Well, as you know, I haven't much ear for music, and I hoped I would get an easy tune; but when my partner, a long, thin, earnest man, with a stutter, burst on me and whistled wildly in my face, I had the hopeless feeling that I had never heard the tune before. In his earnestness he came nearer and nearer, his contortions every moment becoming more extraordinary, his whistling more piercing; and I, by this time convulsed by awful, helpless laughter, could only shrink farther back in my seat and gasp feebly, " Please don't."

Mrs. Crawley was not much better. In my own misery I was aware of her voice saying politely, " I have no idea what the tune is, but you whistle beautifully—quite like a gramophone."

When my disgusted and exhausted partner ceased trying to emulate a steam-engine and began to look human again, I timidly inquired what he had been whistling. " The tune," he replied very stiffly, " was ' Rule, Britannia ! ' "

"Dear me," I replied meekly, "I thought at least it was something from *Die Meistersinger*;" but he deigned no reply and walked away, evidently hating me quite bitterly. I shan't play that game again, and I can't believe the silly man really whistled "Rule, Britannia," for it is a simple tune and one with which I am entirely at home, whereas —but no matter!

G. won by guessing "Annie Laurie." She is splendid at all games, and did I tell you how well she sings? In the cabin, when we are alone, she sings to me snatches of all sorts of songs, grave and gay, but she won't sing in the saloon, where every other woman on board with the smallest pretensions to a voice carols nightly. She is a most attractive person this G., with quaint little whimsical ways that make her very lovable. We are together every minute of the day, and yet we never tire of one another's company. I rather think I do most of the talking. If it is true that to be slow in words is a woman's only virtue, then, indeed, is my state pitiable, for talk I must, and G. is a delightful person to talk to. She listens to my tales of Peter and the others, and asks for more, and shouts with laughter at the smallest joke. I pass as a wit with G., and have a great success.

She is going to stay with a married sister for the
cold weather. Quite like me, only I'm going to
an unmarried brother. I think we are both getting
slightly impertinent to our elders. They tease us
so at meals in the saloon we have to answer back
in self-defence, and it is very difficult to help
trying to be smart ; sometimes, at least with me,
it degenerates into rudeness. I told you about all
the people at our table, but I forgot one—a very
aged man with a long white beard, rather like the
evil magician in the fairy tales, but most harmless.
"Old Sir Thomas Erpingham," I call him, for I
am sure a good soft pillow for that good grey
head were better than the churlish turf of India.
He is very kind, and calls us Sunshine and Brightness, and pays us the most involved Early Victorian
compliments, which we, talking and laughing all
the time, seldom ever hear, and it is left to kind
Mrs. Wilmot to respond.

Nov. 7.

LAST night we had an excitement. We got into
a thick fog and had to stand still and hoot, while
something—a homeward-bound steamer, they say—
nearly ran us down. The people sleeping on deck
said it was most awesome, but I slept peacefully

through it until awakened by an American female running down the corridor and remarking at the top of a singularly piercing voice, "Wal, I am scared!"

To-day·it is beautifully calm and bright; the nasty, hot, damp wind has gone; and we are sitting in our own little corner of the deck, Mrs. Crawley, Mrs Wilmot, G., and I, sometimes reading, sometimes writing, very often talking. It is luck for us to have two such charming women to talk to. Mrs. Crawley is supposed to be my chaperon, I believe I forgot to tell you that Boggley, who is a great friend of hers, wrote and asked her to look after me. How clever of him to fix on one in every way so desirable! Suppose he had asked the Candle!

We have such splendid talks about books. Mrs. Wilmot has, I think, read everything that has been written, also she is very keen about poetry and has my gift—or is it a vice?—of being able to say great pieces by heart, so between us G. is sometimes just a little bored. You see, G. hasn't been brought up in a bookish atmosphere and that makes such a difference. The other night she was brushing her hair, unusually silent and evidently thinking deeply. At last she looked up at me in my bunk, with the brush in her hand and all her hair swept over one shoulder, and said in the most puzzled

way, " What was that nasty thing Mrs Wilmot
was saying all about dead women ? " and do you
know what she objected to ?

> " Deai dead women, with such hair, too,—
> What's become of all the gold
> Used to hang and brush their bosoms ? I
> Feel chilly and grown old "

We are very much worried by people planting
themselves beside us and favouring us with their
views on life in general   One woman—rather a
tiresome person, a spinster with a curiously horse-
like face and large teeth—sometimes stays for hours
at a time and leaves us limp   Even gentle Mrs.
Wilmot approaches, as nearly as it is possible for
her to approach, unkindness in her comments on
her. She has such playful, girlish manners, and
an irritating way of giving vent to the most utter
platitudes with the air of having just discovered a
new truth. She has been with us this morning and
mentioned that her father was four times removed
from a peerage. I stifled a childish desire to ask who
had removed him, while Mrs. Wilmot murmured,
" How interesting ! " As she minced away Mrs.
Crawley said meditatively, " The Rocking Horse
Fly," and with a squeal of delight I realized that
that was what she had always vaguely reminded
me of. You remember the insect, don't you, in

Through the Looking-Glass ? It lived on sawdust.
One lesson one has every opportunity of learning
on board ship is to suffer fools, if not gladly, at
least with patience. The curious people who stray
across one's path! One woman came on at Port
Said—a globe-trotter, globe-trotting alone. Can
you imagine anything more ghastly? She is
very tall, dark and mysterious-looking, and last
night when G. and I were in the music saloon
before dinner, she sat down beside us and began
to talk of spiritualism and other weird things. To
bring her to homelier subjects I asked if she liked
games. " Games," she said, " what sort of games ?
I can ride anything that has four legs and I can
hold my own with a sword " She looked so fierce
that if the bugle hadn't sounded at that moment
I think I should have crept under a table.

" Quite mad," said G. placidly as we left her.

We are going to have a dance to-night.

S S Scotia, Nov. 11.

. . . Now we approach a conclusion. We have
passed Colombo, and in three or four days ought to
reach Calcutta.

Colombo was rather nice, warm and green an
moist ; but I failed to detect the spicy breeze
blowing soft o'er Ceylon's isle, that the hymn led m
to expect. The shops are good and full of interestin
things, like small ivory elephants, silver ornament:
bangles, kimonos, and moonstones. We bough
various things, and as we staggered with our pui
chases into the cabin, which now resembles nothin,
so much as an overcrowded pawnshop, Mr:
Murray remarked (we are on speaking terms again)
" I suppose you thought the cabin looked rathe
empty that you bought so much rubbish to fil
it up."

We were dumb under the deserved rebuke We had
bought her a fan as a peace-offering, rather a pretty
one too, but she thanked us with no enthusiasm.

In Colombo we got rickshaws and drove out to
the Galle Face Hotel, a beautiful place with the
surf thundering on the beach outside. If I were rich
I would always ride in a rickshaw. It is a delight
ful way of getting about, and as we were trotted
along a fine broad road, small brown boys rar
alongside and pelted us with big waxy, sweet
smelling blossoms We did enjoy it so. At the
Galle Face, in a cool and lofty dining-hall, we had
an excellent and varied breakfast, and ate real

proper Eastern curry for the first time. Another new
experience ! I don't like curry at home, curry as
English cooks know it—a greasy make-up of cold
joint served with sodden rice ; but this was different.
First, rice was handed round, every particle firm
and separate and white, and then a rich brown
mixture with prawns and other interesting in-
gredients, which was the curry. You mix the
curry with the rice, when a whole trayful of condi-
ments is offered to eat with it, things like very thin
water biscuits, Bombay duck—all sorts of chutney,
and when you have mixed everything up together
the result is one of the nicest dishes it has been
my lot to taste. Note also, you eat it with a
fork and spoon, not with a fork alone as mere
provincials do !

I begin to feel so excited about seeing Boggley
It is two years since he was home last. Will he
have changed much, I wonder ?   There was a letter
from him at Colombo, and he hadn't left Darjeeling
and had no house to take me to in Calcutta, so it
would appear that when I do land my lodging will
be the cold ground.   It sounds as if he were still the
same casual old Boggley. Who began that name ?
John, I think. He had two names for him—" Lo-
the-poor-Indian " and " Boggley-Wallah "—and in

time we all slipped into calling him Boggley. I like
to think you two men were such friends at Oxford
Long before I knew you I had heard many tales of
your doings, and I think that was one reason why
when we did meet, we liked each other and became
friends, because we were both so fond of Boggley
I am filled with qualms as to whether he will be glad
to see me. It must be rather a nuisance in lots of
ways to have a sister to look after, but he was so
keen that I should come that surely he won't think
me a bother   Besides, when you think of it, it was
really very good of me to leave my home and all my
friends and brave the perils of the deep, to visit a
brother in exile

I wish I knew exactly when we shall arrive ; this
suspense is wearing. One man told me we would
be in on Wednesday, another said we would miss
the tide and not be in till Saturday. I asked the
captain, but he directed me to the barber, who, he
said, knew everything—and indeed there are very
few things he doesn't know. He is a dignified figure
with a shiny curl on his forehead, and a rich Cockney
accent, full of information, generally, I must admit,
strikingly inaccurate, but bestowed with such an
air. " I do believe him though I know he lies."

13th.

WE are in the Hooghly and shall be in Kidder-
pore Dock to-morrow morning early.   Actually the
voyage is at an end.   I may as well finish this letter
and send it with the mail which leaves Calcutta
to-morrow.   We can't pack, because Mrs. Albert
Murray is occupying all the cabin and most of the
passage.   We shall creep down when she is quite
done and put our belongings together.

Everyone is flying about writing luggage labels,
and getting their boxes up from the hold, and counting things.   Curiously enough, I am feeling rather
depressed ; the end of anything is horrid, even a
loathed sea-voyage.   After all, it isn't a bad old ship,
and the people have been nice.   To-night I am
filled with kindness to everyone.   Even Mrs Albert
Murray seems to swim in a rosy and golden haze,
and I am conscious of quite an affection for her,
though I expect, when in a little I go down to the
cabin and find her fussing and accusing us of losing her
things, I shall dislike her again with some intensity.
We have all laughed and played and groaned together, and now we part.   No, I *shan't* say " Ships
that pass in the night."   Several people—mothers
whose babies I have held and others—have given

me their cards and a cordial invitation to go and
stay with them for as long as I like. They mean
it now, I know, but in a month's time shall we even
remember each other's names?

It will be a real grief to part to-morrow from
Mrs Crawley and Mrs. Wilmot. The dear women!
I wish they had been going to stay in Calcutta, but
they go straight away up country. Are there, I
wonder, many such charming women in India?
It seems improbable I shall miss all the people
at our table : we have been such a gay company.
Major Wilmot says G. and I have kept them all
amused and made the voyage pleasant, but that
is only his kind way. It is quite true, though, what
Mrs. Crawley says of G. She is like a great rosy
apple, refreshing and sweet and wholesome.

What is really depressing me is the thought that
wherever I am to-morrow night there will be no G
to say :

" Good-night, my dear. Sleep well "

And I shan't be able to drop my head over my
bunk and reply :

" Good-night, my dear old G."

It will seem so odd and lonely without her.

The ship has stopped—we are to anchor here till
daylight.

FLESHPOTS OF CALCUTTA

In India. I don't think I have quite realized myself or my surroundings yet, but one thing I know. Boggley has been better than his word, for we are not camping in a corner of the Maidan, but have a decent roof to cover us.

But I shall go back to where I left off on Wednesday night.

We spent a hot, breathless night in the river. Towards morning I fell asleep and dreamed that the ship was sinking in a quicksand and that I, in trying to save myself, had stuck fast in the port-hole. I wakened cold with fright, to find it was grey dawn and they were getting up the anchor.

Of course we were up at an unearthly hour, all our belongings carefully packed and labelled, ourselves clad in clean white dresses and topis to face the burning, shining face of India. There was little to see and nothing to do, and we walked about getting hungrier and hungrier, and yet when breakfast-time did come we found we were too excited to eat.

When we got into the dock we saw all the people

who had come to meet us penned like sheep into en-
closures, and we leaned over the side trying to make
out the faces of friends. Presently they were
allowed to come on board, and I, eagerly watching,
spied Boggley bounding up the ladder, and the next
moment we were clutching each other wildly. But
our greeting—what it is to be Scots!—was merely
" Hallo! there you are!" I need not have worried
about what I would say when I met him—yes, I
was silly enough to do that—for he is just the same
dear old Boggley, hair as red, eyes as blue and
as short-sighted, mouth as wide as ever. I think
his legs are even longer. The first thing he did
when he came on board was to fall over someone's
dressing-bag, and that made us both laugh help-
lessly like silly children I introduced him to G.
and the others, and by this time G. had found her
sister, and soon they were all talking together, so G.
and I slipped away to look out for people in whom
we were interested. Very specially did we want
to see Mr. Albert Murray, and when we did see him
he was almost exactly what we had expected—
small, sandy-haired, his topi making his head look
out of all proportion, and with a trodden-on look.
We noticed the little man wandering aimlessly
about, when a voice from the music-room door say-

ing " Albert " made him start visibly, and turning,
he sidled up to our cabin companion, who kissed
him severely, while he murmured, " Well, m' dear,
how are you ? " Seeing us standing near she said,
" Well, good-bye, girls. I hope you'll have a good
time and behave yourselves ; " and then, turning to
her husband, by way of an introduction, she added,
" These are the girls who shared my cabin." Mr.
Albert shuffled his topi and looked at us with kind,
blinking eyes, but attempted no remark. The last
we saw of him he was tugging the hat-box in
the wake of his managing wife. G. looked at me
solemnly. " We had little to complain of," she
said ; " we weren't married to her."

The husband of the Candle was the greatest sur-
prise. I had imagined—why, I don't know—that
that lady's husband would be tall and red-faced,
with a large moustache and loud voice and manner,
someone who would match well with the Candle.
Instead, we beheld a dark, thin-faced man with a
stoop, a man who looked like a scholar and spoke
with a delightful, quiet voice He addressed the
Candle as Jane. *Jane !* If it had been Fluffy, or
Trixie, or Chippy, or even Dolly, but, with that
hair, that complexion, that voice, that troop of
attendant swains, to be called Jane ! The thing

4

was out of all reason. I wonder all the widespread family of Janes, with their meek eyes and smoothly braided hair, don't rise up and call her anything but blessed. Oh, I know there was no thought of pleasing me when she was christened, but still—Jane!

It was rather sweet to watch the little family groups, the mother assuring a bored, indifferent infant that this was its own daddy, and the proud father beaming on both.

The self-conscious bridegrooms sidling up to their blushing brides afforded us much amusement. Some had not seen each other for five years. I wonder if one or two didn't rue their bargains! It seems to me a terrible risk!

I could have gone on watching the people for a long time, but Boggley was anxious to be off; so after tearful farewells and many promises to write had been exchanged, we departed

The special Providence that looks after casual people has guided Boggley to quite a nice house in a nice part of the town. Many Government people who are in Calcutta only for the cold weather—I mean those of them who are burdened not with wealth but women-folk—find it cheaper and more convenient to live in a boarding-house. Does that conjure up to you a vision of Bloomsbury, and tall grey houses, and dirty maid-servants, and the Passing of Third Floor Backs? It isn't one bit like that. This boarding-house consists, oddly enough, of four big houses all standing a little distance apart in a compound. They are let out in suites of rooms, and the occupants can either all feed together in the public dining-room or in lonely splendour in their own apartments. We have five rooms on the ground floor. Of the two sitting-rooms one is almost quite dark, and is inhabited by a suite of furniture, three marble-topped tables on which Boggley had set out the few photographs and trifles which he hasn't yet lost, and a sad-looking cabinet; the other opens into the garden, and is a nice cheerful room The dark room we have made Boggley's study; as he only uses it at night, it doesn't matter about the want of light, and there is a fine large writing-table which holds stacks of papers. We got the marble-topped tables carried into the cheery room and covered them with tablecloths from a shop in Park Street, bought rugs for the floor and hangings for the doors, and with a few cushions and palms and flowers the room is quite pretty and home-like. I like the chairs, enormous cane things with long wooden arms which Boggley says are meant for putting one's feet on, and most comfortable.

Boggley's bedroom is next his study, but I have
to take a walk before I come to mine, out of the
window,—or door, I'm never sure which it is,—
down some steps, then along a garden-walk, round a
corner, and up some more steps, where I reach
first a small ante-room and then my bedroom.
Like the other rooms, it is whitewashed and has a
very high ceiling. Some confiding sparrows have
built a nest in a hole in the wall, and—and this
is really upsetting—there are *ten* different ways of
entering the room, doors and windows, and half of
them I can't lock or bar or fasten up in any way.
What I should do if a Mutiny occurred I can't
think ! My bed with its mosquito-curtains stands
like a little island in a vast sea of matting, and there
are two large wardrobes, what they call *almirahs*,
a dressing-table, and two chairs. It is empty and
airy, and that is all that is required of a bedroom.

The four houses, as I told you, stand in a compound. It isn't exactly a garden, for there are
lots of things in it that we would consider quite
superfluous in a self-respecting garden. There is
a good tennis lawn, plots of flowers, trimly-kept
walks bordered with poinsettias, and trees with
white, heavily-scented flowers, and opposite my
bedroom is a little stone-paved enclosure where

two cows and two calves lead a calm and meditative existence ! And further, there are funny little huts scattered about where one catches glimpses of natives at their devotions or slumbering peacefully. Imagine in the middle of a garden at home coming on a cowhouse or a shanty ! But this is India.

Boggley conducted me round, both of us talking hard all the time. He had so many questions to ask and I had so much to tell : all the home news and silly little home jokes—Peter's latest sayings—things that are so amusing to tell and to hear but lose all their flavour written. You remember Boggley's wild bursts of laughter ? He laughs just the same now, throws his head back and shouts in the most whole-hearted way. We talked from 11 a.m. till tea-time without a break—talked ourselves hoarse and thirsty. After tea we drove on the Maidan, up and down the Red Road in an unending stream of carriages and motors, shabby *tikka-gharries* and smart little dogcarts (called here tum-tums)—all Calcutta taking the air. One might almost have imagined oneself in the Park, if it had not been that now and again a strange equipage would pass filled with natives, men and boys gorgeous in purple and scarlet and gold, or closed carriages like boxes on wheels, in which sat dark-

skinned women demurely veiled. From the Red Road
we drove to the Strand, a carriage-way by the river
where the great ships lie, and watched the sun set
and the spars and masts become silhouetted against
the red sky. Then darkness fell almost at once.

My mind was a chaos when I went to bed after
my first day in India, and I slept so soundly that
when I woke I had no idea where I was. All re-
collections of the voyage and arrival were wiped
from my memory, and I was filled first with vague
astonishment and then with horror to find myself
surrounded by filmy white stuff through which
peered a black face. It was only my *ayah*, a quaint,
small person, wrapped in a white *sari*, with demure,
sly eyes and teeth stained red with chewing betel-
nut, looking through the mosquito-curtains to see if
the Miss Sahib was awake and would like *chota-
hazri*. She embarrasses me greatly slipping about
with her bare feet, appearing when I least expect
her or squatting on the floor staring at me fixedly.
I know no Hindustani and she knows perhaps three
English words, so our conversation is limited. The
silence gets so on my nerves that I drop hairbrushes
and things to make a little disturbance, and it gives
her something to do to pick them up. I must at
once learn some Hindustani words, such as pink,

blue, and green, and then I shall be able to tell Bella what dress to lay out, and her place won't be such a sinecure. I call her Bella because it is the nearest I can get to her name and it has a homely sound.

The rest of my impressions I shall keep for my next letter. I have written this much to give you an idea of my surroundings, and you see I have taken your interest for granted. Are you bored? Of course you will say you are not, but if I could see your face I should know.

The home mail arrives here on Sunday, when people are having what they call a " Europe morning," and have time to read and enjoy their letters. When you wrote you had just had my mail from Marseilles. How far behind you are! It was too bad of me to write such pitiful letters, but I think I was too miserable to pretend   Now I am very well off, and no one could be more utterly thoughtful and kind than old Boggley. I am sure I shall never regret coming to India, and it will be something to dream about when I am a douce Olivia-sit-by-the-fire.

You speak of rain and mud and fog, and it all seems very far away from this afternoon land. The winter will soon pass, and, as you nicely put it, I shall return with the spring.

Calcutta, Nov. 21.

IT is the witching hour of 10 a.m and I am
sitting in my little ante-room—boudoir, call it
what you will—immersed in correspondence.
Boggley, hard-worked man that he is, has departed
for his office followed by a *kitmutgar* carrying some
sandwiches and a bottle of soda-water, which is
his modest lunch   Really a Government servant's
life is no easy one.   He is up every morning by six
o'clock, and gets a couple of hours' work done
before breakfast.   His office receives him at ten
and keeps him till four, when he comes home and
has tea, after which we ride or drive or play tennis
somewhere.   A look in at the Club for a game of
billiards, more work, dinner, and, if we are not
going to a dance or any frivolity, a quiet talk, a
smoke, a few more papers gone through, bed, and
the long Indian day is over.   All day *chuprassis*,
like attendant angels, flit in and out bearing piles
of documents marked Urgent, which they heap
on his writing-table.   I begin greatly to dislike
the sight of them

So you see I have of necessity many hours alone,
at least I have some, and I would have more if G.
didn't live within a few minutes' walk, and every

morning, armed with a large green-lined parasol
and protected by her faithful topi, come round to
pass the time of day with me. Her sister, Mrs.
Townley, is a very nice woman and kindness itself
to me. I can say, like the Psalmist, that goodness
and mercy follow me. I started from London
knowing no one, yet in twenty-four hours I was
fast friends with G. and afterwards with quite a
lot of people on board. I thought when T landed
in Calcutta I would be a stranger in a strange land
and have no one but Boggley, " instead of which "
I have G. quite near, and Mrs. Townley says I
must come to them any minute of the day I want
to ; and there are others equally kind. You don't
want me to give you a detailed account of Calcutta,
do you ? It wouldn't interest you to read it, and
it certainly wouldn't interest me to write it. When
my friends go wandering and write me home long
descriptions of the places of interest (falsely so
called) which they visit, I read them—oh ! I read
them faithfully—but I am sadly bored. Somehow
people interest me more than places. That being
so, I shall only inflict on you a little of Calcutta.
I like it immensely. They laugh at me for saying
it is pretty, but I do think it is quite beautiful.
It is so much greener than I expected, and I like

the broad streets of pillared houses standing in their palm-shaded compounds. The principal street is called Chowringhee, and it has some fine buildings and really excellent shops, where one can buy quite as pretty things as in London, only, of course, they are of necessity more expensive ; it costs a lot to bring them out. The Clubs are in this street, the Bengal Club, and the United Service where my brother would even now be leading a comfortable bachelor existence if he hadn't had a bothering sister to provide a habitation for.

Chowringhee faces the Maidan, a very large park containing among other things a race-course, and cricket and football grounds. The word Maidan is Arabic and Persian and Hindustani for an open space, and I hope you like the superior way I explain things to you. You, who can be silent in so many languages, will probably know what Maidan means —but no matter.

This, then, is the European Calcutta, clean and spacious and pleasant, but not nearly so interesting as the native part   Turn down a side street, walk a little way and you are in a nest of mean streets, unpaved, dirty, smelling vilely, lined with open booths, where squat half-naked men selling lumps of sticky sweetmeats and piles of things

that look like unbaked scones and other strange
eatables ; and little naked babies tumble in the
dust with goats and puppies. It seems to me
that I go about asking " Why ? " all day and no
one gives me a satisfactory answer to anything.
Why, for example, should we require a troop of
servants living, as we do, in a kind of hotel ?   And
yet there they are—Boggley's bearer and my
ayah—I can see some reason for their presence—
a *kitmutgar* to wait on us at table and bring tea
in   the   afternoon, another young   assistant *kitmutgar* who scurries like a frightened rabbit at my
approach, a delightful small boy who rejoices in the
name of *pani-wallah*, whose sole duty is to carry
water for the baths, the *dhobi* who washes our
clothes by beating them between two large—and
I should say, judging by the state of the clothes,
sharp—stones, losing most of them in the process,
and a *syce* or groom for each pony.   Seated, as one
sometimes sees them, in rows on the steps, aug-
mented by a *chuprassi* or two, brilliant in uniform,
they make a sufficiently imposing spectacle.   I
have few words, but I look at them in as pleasant
a way as I know how, partly because I like to be
friends with servants, and partly because I'm rather
afraid of them and don't want to rouse them to

Mutiny or do anything desperate, but Boggley discouraged me at the outset "You needn't grin at them so affably," he remarked, "they will only think you are weak in the head." They quite evidently regard me as a poor creature, even Bella, though she humours me and condescends to say "pretty pretty," or "nicey nicey" when I am dressed in the evening I think she must once have nursed children, for the words she knows are baby words; she always calls me "poor Missy baba" and strokes me! The *pani-wallah* finds amusement in practising his English on me. When he sees G. come through the compound, he bounds to my room, holds up the *chick* and announcing "Mees come," retires, stiff with pride at his knowledge of the language.

I have learned a few useful Hindustani words. *Qui hai* means roughly, "Is anyone there?" and you cry that instead of ringing a bell, and it brings the instant response "*Huzoor*," and a servant springs from nowhere to do your bidding. *Lao* means "bring" and *Jao* "go." You never say "please," and you learn the words in a cross tone—that is, if you want to be really Anglo-Indian. Radical M.P.'s of course will learn "please" at once, if there is such a word in the language, which I doubt. One nice globe-trotting old lady, anxious, like me, to conciliate the natives, was having a cup of chocolate at Peliti's, and she insisted on sending out to see if the *tikka-gharry wallah* would like a cup !

A *tikka-gharry* is a thing like a victoria, hired by the hour. There are first, second, and third class *tikka-gharries.* The first class have two horses, the second one horse, and the third is closed, and, having no springs, is a terrible vehicle indeed. The drivers of these carriages have, as a rule, long whiskers, and are dressed in khaki. They have bags of provender for the horses tied behind the conveyance, where also precariously hangs another man who might be the twin-brother of the driver. I don't know why he is there, but there he is.

G. and I love to set out in a *tikka-gharry* and practise our Hindustani. Starting early when it is fairly cool—Indian cold weather mornings are the most wonderful things, so fresh and so bright and so blue—G. starts us off at a mad gallop by shouting *Juldi jao*, which I have to calm down with *Asti asti* (slower). When we reach Peliti's we cry *Roko* (stop), and get out to buy caramels, chocolates, and cakes for tea. Peliti has a peculiarly delicious kind of chocolate cake, the recipe for which I wish

he would confide to Fuller or Buszard. But it
isn't the European shops, good as they are, that
occupy our mornings Much more fascinating
haunts await us, the New Market and the China
Bazaar. The former is a kind of arcade which
contains everything that any reasonable person
could require; fragrant fruit and flowers, fresh-
smelling vegetables, and the wares of butcher and
baker and candlestick-maker, all laid out on booths
and stalls for the world to choose from.

There, very early in the morning, come the
khansamahs of the various Mem-sahibs and buy all
that is needed for the day, while the Mem-sahibs
are cosy in bed, needing not to worry about house,
visitors, or forthcoming dinner-parties House-
keeping is easy in India. Boggley thought we had
better ask some people to dinner, so we did, though
I pointed out that we had no silver or anything to
make the table decent ; and the boarding-house
things are none too dainty. " It'll be all right," said
Boggley, " leave it to the servants ; " so I engaged
the private dining-room—and left it. I rather
trembled whe the evening came and our party
walked in, but I needn't have. The servants were
worthy of their trust. The table looked charming,
and, as I had never seen any of the things before,

I had a more interesting time than usually falls
to the hostess. What I sincerely hoped was that
none of the guests had seen any of the things before
either, but if they had they possessed great control
of their countenances.

Eatables, however, are by no means the only
things to be found in the New Market. Silks,
muslins, chicon-work, silver ornaments, and jewellery
keep us breathless, while the pleasant shopman in
a frock-coat and turban offers them at what he
calls " killin' " prices.

The China Bazaar is much farther into the city,
quite in the native quarter. It is a real adventure
to make an expedition there, and the owners allow
us to poke in back rooms from which we unearth
wondrous treasures in the way of old brass vases ;
queer, slender - necked scent - bottles still faintly
smelling of roses ; old lacquer boxes, and bits of
rich embroidery. I am becoming a Shylock in the
way I beat down prices. I shouldn't wonder a bit
when I go home and am ruffling it once more in
Bond Street if, when told the price of a thing is a
guinea, I laugh in a jocular way and say, " Oh !
come now, I'll give you ten shillings."

But to return to Hindustani. I haven't told you
all I know. I can ask for *tunda* beef, which is cold

beef, just as *tunda pani* is cold water, *gurrum pani*
being hot ! I can order what I want at meals At
first when I wanted boiled eggs and heard Boggley
order *unda bile*, I remonstrated, " Not under-boiled,
hard-boiled," until it was explained to me that
unda meant egg. The native can't say any word
beginning with *s* without putting a *y* before it,
thus—y-spice beef, y-street. When men come to
see us I cry, " *Qui hai ?*" and, when the servant
appears, order " *Peg lao—cheroot lao,*" and feel
intensely Anglo-Indian and rather fast. One trait
the language has which appeals greatly to me is
that one can spell it almost any way one likes, but
that is enough about Hindustani for one letter.

23rd.

I HAVE come in from a ride with Boggley. The
proper time to ride is early morning, but I am too
lazy and too timid to go when the place is crowded,
and so we ride in the cool of the evening, when we
have the race-course almost to ourselves I ride
one of Boggley's polo ponies, Solomon by name.
Boggley says he is as quiet as a lamb, but I am
not sure that he is speaking the strict truth ; he
has some nasty little ways, it seems to me. He

bites for one thing. We were riding with a man the other night and quite suddenly his pony got up in the air and nearly threw him. *Solomon had bitten him.* The man looked at me as if it were my fault, and I regret to say I laughed. He has also an ungentlemanly way of trying to rub me off against the railings, and then again, for no apparent reason, he suddenly scurries wildly across the Maidan while I pull desperately, but impotently, with fingers weak from fright. Boggley coming behind convulsed with laughter, merely remarks that I am a *funk-stick*—which, I take it, means the worst kind of coward.

29th.

THINK where I have been for the last three days! Down the river in a launch. That kind Mrs. Townley was taking G. and asked Boggley if I might go. We had to leave on Saturday morning before seven to catch the tide, so I warned Bella that she must bring my *chota-hazri* before six; but I woke and found it was after six, and there were no signs of the perfidious little black Bella. I wasn't nearly ready when G rushed in, but I threw on garments and we fled, while Boggley, in his

5

dressing-gown, followed with a parting benediction
of Peliti's cake as a substitute for tea and toast.
We found the launch delightfully comfortable,
not to say luxurious. It had been done up for
some of the royalties who were out here. There
were only we three on board and three young sailor
men, so it was a blessedly peaceful three days.
We lay on deck and watched the life of the river,
all the ships a-sailing, big ships from Dundee and
Greenock, German ships, French ships, every kind
and nationality of ships down to the curious native
craft. Sometimes we passed a little village on the
river-bank with a temple and an idol on a mound.
When we anchored in the afternoon two of the
officers went on shore to shoot, and the sailors let
down a net and caught delicious fish for dinner.
I did wish Peter had been there. He would have
felt like Robinson Crusoe and rejoiced in it all.
At dinner the young men told us wonderful stories
of their adventures with snakes and tigers. One
man said that he was having his bath one morning
when a snake came up the pipe. When it saw
him it went down again, but as it was disappearing
he pulled it back by its tail. Again it tried to go
down and again he pulled it back, and then the
snake took a look at him and went down tail first.

I believed every word, but when I came home and related the amazing tales to Boggley he received them with derisive shouts of laughter, and said they had been spinning us sailors' yarns.

The mail was waiting here when I came back yesterday. Thanks so much for your letter. I am immensely interested in all your news, but I have left myself no time to answer you properly, as this must be posted to-day.

N.B—The two queerest things I have noticed in Calcutta up to now are :

(*a*) That when a man goes out to tennis and stays to dinner his bearer carries his dress-clothes *wrapped in a towel*.

(*b*) Kippered herrings come to the table *rolled up in paper*.

Calcutta, Dec. 2.

I DON'T think I like this casting of bread upon the water ; I never know which loaf it is I am receiving again. You reply to things I had forgotten I had written, and it is rather bewildering.

When you get this you will be settled down in

Germany. I am sorry you have left London for
one reason, and that a purely selfish one. I shan't
be able to imagine you in your new surroundings,
and in London I knew pretty well what you would
be doing every minute of the day. Knowing, as
we do, many of the same people, when you wrote
" I have been dining with the Maxwell-Tempests
to meet the So-and-sos," I could picture it all even
to little Mrs. Maxwell-Tempest's attitudes. I was
only in Germany once for three days, and I came
away with an impression of a country weird as to
food, feathery as to beds, and crammed full of
soldiers ; but I dare say it is a very good place to
write a book. And now—my heartiest congratula-
tions on having a book to write. It sounds—
pardon me for saying it—a very dull subject, but
if I were a little wiser I expect I should see how
important it is, and anyway I have enough sense
to perceive that it is a great compliment to be
asked to write it. What fun to be a man and have
a career ! In my more exalted moments it is
sometimes borne in on me that I should have been
a man and a diplomatist. I feel, though I admit
with no grounds to speak of, that I might have
been a great success in that most interesting profession. One never knows, and by putting my

foot in it very conscientiously all round, I might
have earned for myself a reputation of Machiavellian
cunning !

What do you think I met at dinner last night ?
A Travelling Radical Member of Parliament !

Of course I had read of them—often—and knew
exactly what sort of creatures they are—fearful
wild fowl who come to India for six weeks—

> "Comprehend in half a mo'
> What it takes a man ten years or so
> To know that he will never know,"

tell the native they want to be a brother to him,
and go home to write a book about the way India is
misgoverned.

I was delighted at the prospect of seeing one quite
close at hand. I pictured a strong still man with a
beard, soft fat hands, and a sob in his voice that, at
election times, would touch the great, deep throb-
bing Heart of the People. Instead, I beheld a
small, thin man, with eyes as tired as any of the
poor sun-dried bureaucrats, and a wide mouth with
a humorous twitch at the corners ; a man one
couldn't imagine wanting to touch anything so
silly as the Heart of the People. He talked, I
noticed, very little during dinner, but the men were
unusually long in joining us afterwards, and as

Boggley clambered after me into the *tikka-gharry*
that was to take us home : " That's a ripping
fellow ! " said Boggley.

Another illusion shattered !

I hasten to set your mind at rest on one point.
I have a chaperon, and a very nice, though entirely
unnecessary, one. Her name is Mrs. Victor
Ormonde, and she knows my people at home ;
that is why she bothers with me. She is a most
attractive woman to look at, tall, dark and slender,
with the dearest little turned-up nose, which makes
her look rather impertinent, and she is a little
inclined to be sniffy to some people ; she considers
Calcutta women suburban ! Her husband is quite
different, friends with everyone, a cheerful soul
and as Irish as he can be. He is very fond of
chaffing his exclusive wife. " Now do be affable,"
he implored her the other night, before they went
to a large and somewhat mixed gathering. " And
was she affable ? " I asked next morning. " Oh !
rollin' about on the floor," was the obviously untrue
reply.

You ask how I like the Anglo-Indian women,
and I don't know quite what to say. It is the old
story. When they are nice they are very, very
nice, but when they are nasty they are *horrid*

Some of them I simply hate. They give me such nasty little stabs the while they smile and pretend to be pleasant !

I am quite capable of giving back as good as I get, but it isn't worth while, because if one does yield to the temptation, afterwards one feels such a worm. There is no doubt it is more difficult in India than at home to obey the command of one's childhood : " to behave pretty and be a lady." What is a lady exactly ? I used to be told that a lady was one who always said " please " when asking for more bread-and-butter, and who never bit the fingers of her gloves. That was simple " And what'll I be if I'm not a lady ? " I asked. " You'll be common," said the nurse severely, and then and there, because snatched bread-and-butter was sweet and gloves chewed in secret pleasant, I registered a vow that common I would be. A dear little lady I met the other day, talking about her sister Memsahibs, said airily, " Of course we very soon lose complexions, manners, and morals." She could afford to say so, it being so obviously untrue in her case. I think it is just this, that the women who are pure gold grow more charming, but the pinchbeck wears off very soon. The Eastern sun reveals blemishes, moral and physical, that would pass

unnoticed in the murkier atmosphere of England.
The wonder to me is that anyone keeps nice when
one thinks of the provocation there is to deteriorate.
The climate, the lack of any serious occupation
to take up their days, the constant round of gaieties
indulged in partly, I believe, to keep themselves
from thinking, the ever-present anxiety about the
children at home—oh! there is much one could
say if one held a brief for the Anglo-Indian women.

Calcutta society is made up of Government
people, Army people, and business people who are
called, for some unknown reason, *box-wallahs*.
It seems very strange that there should be such
a desire to go one better than one's neighbour,
to have better horses, a smarter carrriage, a larger
house, smarter gowns, because, at least in the case
of the Civil Service people, their income is known
down to the last rupee.

Everybody in India is, more or less, somebody.
It must be a very sad change to go home to England
and be (comparatively) poor and shabby, and certainly obscure, to have people remark vaguely
they suppose you are "something in India." I
suppose we are all snobs at heart. Snobbery,
sir, doth walk about the orb like the sun, it shines
everywhere. A good lady talked to me quite

seriously lately about what the Best People in
Calcutta did. It has become a light table joke
with us, and when I plant my elbows on the table
and hum a tune while we are waiting for the next
course at dinner, Boggley mildly inquires, "Do the
Best People do that?"

It is a subject I never gave much attention to,
but now awful doubts assail me. Am I the Best
People? One thing is certain : I am of very little
importance. I am only a *chota* Miss Sahib and my
chota-ness is my great protection. No one is going
to bother much what I do, or trouble to pull my
clothes and my conduct to pieces, and I can creep
along unnoticed to a great extent ; I watch the game
and find it vastly entertaining.

It grieves me to say that I am one of the class who
ought to remain in England. There I am quite a
nice person up to my lights, fairly unselfish, loving
my neighbour as myself. But I have proved myself
pinchbeck. No, you needn't say I'm sweet, I'm not.
I find myself saying the most detestable things about
people. Oblivious of the beam in my own eye, I
stare fixedly and reprovingly at the mote in my
neighbour's. Could anything be more unlovable?

I get no encouragement to be a cat from Boggley.
Everyone is his very good friend.

" Mrs. Wright called to-day," I remark at tea.

" Did she ? " says Boggley. " She's a nice little woman ; you'll like her."

" She makes up," I say, " and she had on a most ridiculous hat. Mrs. Brodie says she's a dreadful flirt."

" Rubbish ! " says Boggley ; " she's a very good sort and devoted to her husband."

" Mrs. Brodie says," I continue, " that she is horrid to other women and tries to take away their husbands. It *is* odd how fond Anglo-Indian women are of other people's husbands."

" Much odder," Boggley retorts, " that you should have become such a little backbiting cat ! You'll soon be as bad as old Mother Brodie, and *she's* the worst in Calcutta "

This is the Christmas mail, and I have written sixteen letters, but I can't send presents except to Mother and some girls, for I haven't seen a single thing suitable for a man. Poor Peter wailed for a monkey or a mongoose, but I told him to wait till I came home and I would do my best to bring one or both.

I can only send you greetings from a far country.

You know you will never be better than I wish you.

Calcutta, Dec. 10.

DEAR MR. OLIVER TWIST,—I really don't think
I can write longer letters. They seem to me very
long indeed. I am not ashamed of their length,
but I am ashamed, especially when I read yours, of
their dullness and of the poverty-stricken attempt
at description. How is it that you can make your
little German town fascinating, when I can only
make this vast, stupefying India sound dull ? It
wouldn't sound dull if I were telling you about it
by word of mouth. I could make you see it then ;
but what can a poor uninspired one do with a pen,
some ink, and a sheet of paper ?

I have been employing a shining hour by paying
calls. You must know that in India the new
arrival does not sit and wait to be called on, she
up and calls first. It is quite simple. You call your
carriage—or, if you haven't aspired to a carriage,
the humble, useful *tikka-gharry*—and drive away
to the first house on the list, where you ask the
durwan at the gate for *bokkus*. If the lady is not
receiving, he brings out a wooden box with the in-
scription " Mrs What's-her-name Not at home,"
you drop in your cards, and drive on to the next.
If the box is not out, then the *durwan*, taking the

cards, goes in to ask if his mistress is receiving, and comes back with her salaams, and that means that one has to go in for a few minutes, but it doesn't often happen. The funny part of it is one may have hundreds of people on one's visiting list and not know half of them by sight, because of the convenient system of the "Not-at-home" box.

The men's calling-time is Sunday between twelve and two. Such a ridiculous time! One is certainly not at one's best at that hour. Isn't it the Irish R.M. who talks of that blank time of day when breakfast has died within one and lunch is not yet? I find it, on the whole, entertaining, though somewhat trying; for Boggley, you see, has to be out paying calls on his own account, and so I have to receive my visitors alone. It is quite like a game.

A servant comes in and presents me with a card inscribed with a name unfamiliar, and I, saying something that sounds like "Salaam do," wait breathless for what may appear. A man comes in. We converse.

I begin: "Where will you sit?" (As there are only four chairs in the room, the choice is not extensive)

THE MAN (*seated and twirling his hat*): "You have just come out?"

MYSELF: " Yes, in the *Scotia.*"   Remarks follow about the voyage

THE MAN . " What do you think of India ? "

MYSELF: " Oh, rather nice, don't you think ? "

THE MAN . " Oh, quite a decent place—what ? "

Again the servant appears, this time with two cards. Again I murmur the Open Sesame, and two more men appear. No. 1 gets up to go, shakes hands with me in a detached way, and departs, and the same conversation begins again with the new-comers, until they, in their turn, leave when someone else comes in. It seems to be etiquette to go away whenever another visitor arrives. I didn't understand this, and when a man came whom I knew well in my childhood's days and, after a few minutes' stay, got up to depart, I grabbed his hand and said, " Oh, won't you stay and have a talk ? " He, very nicely, stayed on, and we did have a delightful talk ; but Victor Ormonde, who happened to be present, has never ceased to chaff me about it. When we dine with them and get up to go he says in thrilling accents, with an absurdly sentimental air, " Oh ! *won't* you stay and have a talk ? "

I do think India makes very nice men. Almost every man I have met has been delightful in his own

way. . . . I had just written that last sentence
when a servant brought in a card inscribed " Colonel
Simpson." I got my sunshade and walked round
to my sitting-room, where I found a tall, pensive-
looking man. Thinking he must be a friend of
Boggley's, I held out my hand frankly, and having
shaken it, the man went on holding it.

Like Captain Hook, I murmured to myself, " This
is unusual," but I tried to conceal my astonishment,
and we sat down together on the sofa. Then he
began to *feel my pulse* By this time I had made
up my mind he must be a lunatic, and I had a wild
idea of snatching away my hand and making a
bound for the window ; but feeling that my legs
were too weak with fright to be of any real use to
me, I remained seated.

" Are you sick ? " he asked.

" Not in the least, thank you," I stammered.

A doubtful look flickered over his pensive
countenance.

" Are you not my patient ? " he asked.

" No," I answered truthfully.

" But—I was sent for to a Mrs. Woodward ;
this .was the address, and I was shown in
here."

He was so upset that I hastened to assure him

it did not matter in the least ; that Mrs. Woodward lived above us, and it was quite, quite all right. But my comforting protestations profited nothing, and the poor man retired in great confusion, murmuring incoherently. If I had seen "doctor" on his card I might have been prepared, but who would expect a Colonel to be a doctor ? This confusing India !

Later.

This has been a queer day! Nothing but alarums and excursions. G came to tea and suggested that afterwards we should go for a drive in a *tikka-gharry*, it being a more amusing mode of conveyance in G.'s eyes than her sister's elegant carriage. So we drove up and down the Red Road and along the Strand until the darkness came. It rained this morning—the first rain I have seen in this dusty land—making the roads quite muddy and the air damp and cold.

"It's like an evening in England," said G. "Let's get out and walk home." So we told the driver to *roko*, and G., who had the money to pay him in her hand, got out first ; at least I thought she was out, but she had paused, balanced on the step, and my slight push knocked her headlong. How

she did it I don't know, but her feet remained in
the *gharry*, while her head was in close conjunction
to the horses' hoofs. I suppose astonishment at
this feat must have numbed my finer feelings, for
G. insists I bounded over her prostrate form,
grabbed the money from her hand, and paid the
man before I even inquired if she were killed.
When I had time to look at her I was glad it was
getting dark, and that we were in an unfrequented
road. Her white serge costume was mud from
head to foot, her hat was squashed out of shape,
and even her poor face bore traces of contact with
the Red Road. At first she couldn't rise, not
because she was hurt, but because she was helpless
with laughter. When I did get her on her feet, I
found the only injury was a slight cut on the wrist,
and great was my relief.

It was a blessing that no native reporters were
near, or to-morrow morning we would see in large
letters : SHOCKING AFFAIR IN THE RED ROAD.
ONE EUROPEAN LADY ATTACKS ANOTHER.

My only fear was tetanus. We have been told
such tales of a slight cut causing death that I hurried
G along until we burst breathless into a chemist's
shop in Park Street and demanded " something to
keep away tetanus ! "

The chemist gave us some permanganate of potash, and for the last hour I have been bathing he wrist, assisted by Bella, who has ruined two of my best handkerchiefs in the process. The damaged ʒ. has just departed, and I do hope won't be much he worse. Such awful things happen here. You meet people well and strong one day and hear of heir death the next. Death seems appallingly near. One isn't given time to be ill Either you are quite well or else you are dead

Now I must stop and go and dress, I see Bella fidgeting. When this reaches you the Old Year will be very near its end I hate to let it go : it has been such a good old year Is it that I forget the unpleasant parts? Perhaps, but in looking back I seem to remember only sunny days and pleasant things

To you, my friend, I send every possible good wish for the New Year. May it be the best you have ever had May it bring you health, wealth, and, above all, happiness.

> "The world is so full of a number of things,
> I am sure we should all be as happy as kings."

Isn't that a lovable sentiment ?

6

I AM trying to take an interest in Germany and
the Germans for your sake, but, as I told you before,
Germany is a place I know little or nothing about.
France—that noble, fine land—I know and love well.
Italy I should like better if there were not so many
Madonnas and Children (or ought I to say Madonnas
and Childs ?) to look at ; Switzerland is my darling
own place, but Germany I have hitherto only
associated with Goethe whom as a poet I dislike,
large sausages, and theological doubts. Your description makes me feel that I may have misjudged
the country and the people ; in fact, your little
town sounds a most attractive place to live in. No,
I don't think I would expect you to make friends
easily. I think you are the sort of man to have
hosts of acquaintances and only one or two real
friends. You know, you rather scare people. I
think it is partly your manner and greatly your
monocle ; you have such a detached air, and often
I have noticed you very unresponsive when people
were trying to be amusing. Oh, I don't mean
you are ever rude, but you are sometimes chilling.
If I hadn't known from Boggley that you were, as
he puts it, a perfect jewel, I think I should have

shrunk away from before you that first day we met
and sat next each other at lunch. I remember I
talked a great deal of nonsense, partly, I think,
because I was rather afraid of you ; and somehow
or other we have always gone on talking nonsense
to each other since. It has become a habit.

But you don't really want to have a great crowd
of friends, do you ? It is only weak-minded people
like myself who flop on any stranger's neck with
protestations of undying affection. It is the easiest
thing in the world for any Douglas that ever was
to make friends : I think because we are always
willing to laugh at the feeblest jest. Nothing
endears one so quickly to one's fellow-beings as
laughing at their jokes. We have a way, too,
of making friends with any casual stranger we
may meet in trains, or coach, or steamer. You
superior people, who, ignoring your fellow-passengers,
sit in a corner and read *The Spectator*, don't know
what you miss. The thrilling stories I have listened
to ! Once I heard a circumstantial story of a
wreck in the South Seas told by the plucky little
wife of the captain, who had stayed by her husband's
side—" Papa " she called him—while the ship
slowly sank on a coral reef, and then drifted about
in an open boat for days before they were rescued.

It is Mother, however, who meets with the oddest
adventures travelling. One day last summer I
saw her off in the Scotch Express from Euston,
comfortably seated in a corner with books and
papers, expecting she would have a nice quiet day.
The occupant of the other corner was a Russian
lady, and the friend who saw her off asked Mother
if she would see she had lunch all right, for she knew
no English. This Mother readily promised, and the
train started. Mother tried once or twice to speak
to the creature, but, receiving only grunts in reply,
began a book. She hadn't read the first chapter
when the old gentleman opposite said sternly,
" Your friend is fainting," and turning, Mother was
just in time to catch the Russian as she slid to the
floor. She wrestled with her for an hour, reviving
her with smelling-salts, and making her comfortable
with her air-cushion and rug, distracted all the time
by the yelling of young infants somewhere near.
As soon as she could leave her she went to see what
was wrong, and found twin-babies making day
hideous with their din, while their poor mother
lay stretched on a seat, too ill to cope with
them.

She was a missionary's wife, it turned out, on
her way home, with no nurse and much malaria,

so, of course, Mother had to stay and nurse the twins until luncheon was ready, when another Good Samaritan came and took a turn. While having luncheon she was hailed by a friend, lately left a widow, who insisted on Mother accompanying her to her compartment, where she wept on her shoulder while telling her all the details of her husband's last illness ; then back again to nurse the Russian and the babies until the journey's end, when she emerged almost as hot, and crumpled, and exhausted as if she had run behind all the way.

How heartily, my friend, I agree with you about the tiresomeness of balls. I think it must be old age approaching, but I can't see any use in going off at the hour when, under happier circumstances, I would be thinking of bed, to a hot, crowded ballroom ; and just at present Calcutta is simply congested with balls. I don't like things that cost a lot ; simple little pleasures please me much more. To drive out to Tollygunge of an afternoon, have tea and a game of croquet, look at the picture papers, and come quietly home again, is to me the height of bliss.

Tollygunge is a club, some miles out of Calcutta, with a race-course, golf-links, croquet-lawns—a very delectable spot. The correct thing is to drive out on Sunday morning and have breakfast out in the open air. Then one sees everyone one knows, and it is very gay; but I think it is much pleasanter to drive out quietly in the afternoon.

The road to Tollygunge lies partly through the jungle, past clusters of native huts where little chocolate-coloured babies roll and chatter in the sunlit dust. You know, the jungle is quite near Calcutta. When I lie at nights and listen to the jackals howling, I remember Kipling's story, and wonder if we were driven out and the jungle were let in, how long it would be before Calcutta became a habitation for the beasts of the field.

Yesterday I drove out with Mrs. Townley and G., and three tired people we were, too tired even to play the gentle game of croquet; glad to sit still in comfortable chairs on the greensward and steep ourselves in the peace and quietness.

At tea, Chil the kite, hovering in mid-air, watched us jealously. Suddenly there was a swoop, a dark flutter of wings, a startled squeak from G., and our cake was gone. That's India !

Tea finished, while we still sat loath to leave, a curious odour forced itself upon our attention. G. sniffed   *I* sniffed. " Whatever is it ? " asked G. Mrs. Townley pointed riverwards to where a thin column of blue-grey smoke rose and hung like a cloud in the hot, still air.

"It's a burning ghat," she said. "They are burning a body"

And *that* is India!

When one is feeling fairly peaceful and secure, something ghastly, like the smell of burning Hindoo, recalls to one the uncertainty of all things We rose to go home, feeling depressed, the smell pursuing us.

I have two pieces of news for this letter

First, Boggley can take a few days' holiday at Christmas, so he means to take me to Darjeeling to see if we can catch a glimpse of the snows. We shall only be there from Saturday afternoon till Monday at noon, and Boggley says that Kangchenjunga is often cloud-covered for weeks, so it is a mere chance whether we shall see it. But surely, surely Kangchenjunga won't be coy with me. I came to India, of course, in the first place to see Boggley, but in the second place to see the snows, and I can't believe that the gods will be so unkind as to deny a humble worshipper of great mountains a sight of the vision glorious.

The other piece of news is quite important.

Boggley has got a new billet. What it is I shan't

try to explain, for I don't understand the game of General Post which is played so frequently among Government officials, but it means that he will have to go on a tour of inspection all over everywhere, and, what is more, I shall go too.   Isn't it fine ?

Boggley actually hesitated about accepting, because he thought I should so hate to leave Calcutta and its gaieties to wander in the jungle   It isn't that I don't enjoy Calcutta ; I do, and I am most grateful to the people who have given me such a good time ; but I pine to see something of the real India.   Calcutta might be a suburb of London.   I want to see the native of India, not the fat babu ; I want to live in tents and be a gipsy ; I want to have Boggley all to myself   We have hardly time at present to pass the time of day with each other.

Boggley tries to frighten me with tales of dâk-bungalows and jungly cooking, but I won't be frightened ; I am looking forward to it all too much.

We don't go till the beginning of January, so I shall be able to attend the Drawing-Room and a few other *tamashas* before we depart.

This will have to do for a letter this week.   I must clean some gloves now   That is the only useful thing I do, clean G.'s gloves and my own   We dirty

so many pairs of long white gloves, and it is cheaper
to clean them at home You do it with petrol and
a small piece of flannel, and the result isn't bad,
though somewhat streaky. G 's part is to sit on
my bed and watch me do it, assisted by Bella on
the floor. It reminds me of the inhabitants of the
Scilly Islands, who, it is said, earn a precarious live-
lihood by taking in each other's washings !

Calcutta, Dec. 26.

WHEN Kipling wrote his *Christmas in India* I
think he must have been in a dâk-bungalow down
with fever, otherwise he would hardly have painted
such a very gloomy picture. I, at least, didn't find
it a mocking Christmas—but then India isn't my
grim stepmother, as Victor Ormonde pointed out
to me the other night. I can afford to be home-
sick, can afford to let myself think of the " black
dividing sea and alien plain," because here I have
no continuing city. It is the real exiles," shackled
in a lifelong tether," who may not think, but must
go doggedly through their day's darg.

I found it an agreeable day, from the morning

when I got my presents and various offerings of flowers, to the evening, when we dined with some very kind people, and had an amusing time playing childish games.

I have often seen pictures headed "Christmas in the Tropics," and looked with sentimental eyes at the people grouped among palm-trees on a verandah, while the girl at the piano sang what was evidently a song about " the dear homeland," to judge from the far-away look in the eyes of all present. It seems a pity to disillusion you, but it isn't at all like that To begin with, it was quite chilly, and we were very glad of the big fire burning in the grate, and we did not look pensive or far-away, but ate our dinner with great content. I think, perhaps, Christmas fare is even more uninteresting in India than at home ; turkey tastes more like white flannel, and plum-pudding is stodgier, and there are no white and scarlet berries or robins ; but otherwise it is really a nicer day than in England.

Of course I thought a lot about the home people. I imagined Peter waking and groping for his stocking. Oh, *have* you forgotten what it felt like to waken up and remember it was Christmas morning ? I sometimes wish I could still hang up my stocking. There is nothing in Grown-up Land that equals the thrill the delicious bulginess of the stocking, gripped in the darkness, gave one.

I think they would miss me a little at home. I know Mother would often say, " I wonder what Olivia is doing now ! "

And what kind of Christmas had you ? A very festive one, I hope.

Very many thanks for the book you sent me. You couldn't possibly have given me anything I like better. Somehow, I have never possessed a copy of *A Child's Garden of Verses*, and this one, so exquisitely, specially bound, will be a great treasure. I like, too, your reason for choosing it. It is nice of you to like my childish reminiscences, but it is rash to say you wish you had known us then. Looking at us now, so quiet, so well-behaved, *such* ornaments to society, you would be surprised what villains we once were—at least on week-days ! We had what R L. S. calls a " covenanting childhood." Looking back, it seems to me that our childhood was a queer mixture of Calvinism and fairy tales. Calvinism, even now, I associate with ham and eggs—I suppose because Sabbath morning was the only time we ever tasted that delicacy. Between bustling Saturday night, when we wistfully watched our toys being locked away, and cheery Monday morning,

when things began again, there was a great gulf
fixed, and that was the Sabbath Day. What strenuous Sabbath Days we had ! First there was worship
and the Catechism. (The only time I ever wished
to be English was when I thought I might have
dallied with " What is your name ? " instead of
wrestling with such deep things as " What is man's
chief end ? ") After worship was over we were
allowed to walk in the garden till it was time for the
morning service. That was the Forenoon Diet of
Worship, then came the Afternoon Diet of Worship.
Having sat like rocks through them both, we proceeded to the Sabbath School, and then went home
to tea, and cake, and jam, and an evening filled with
bound volumes of *The Christian Treasury*, where we
wrestled with tales of religious bigotry and perse-
cution until we seemed to breathe the very atmosphere of dark and mouldy cells, and became
daringly familiar with the thumb-screw and the
rack, the Inquisition and other devildoms of Spain.
I used to wonder pitifully why it had never
occurred to the poor victims to say their prayers
in bed, and thus save themselves such fiery
trials

I wonder why I pretend we found our Sundays a
trial. Looking back, I love every minute of them.

Father could make any day delightful ; and what a through-the-week Father he was ! Sometimes he came to tea with us in the nursery and made believe there was a fairy called Annabel Lee in the teapot, carrying on conversations with her that sent eerie thrills down our several spines. Afterwards he would read out of a little green and gold book that contained for us all the romance of the ages between its elegant covers. From Father we heard of Angus the Subtle, Morag of the Misty Waỹ, and the King of Errin, who rides and rides and whose road is to the End of Days. Sometimes, laying books aside, he told us old tales that he had heard from his mother, who in turn had heard them from hers— of the Red Etain of Ireland who lived in Belligand, and who stole the King's daughter, the King of fair Scotland ; and the pathetic tale of the bannock that went to see the world, with its cynical end : " Ah, well ! We'll all be in the tod's hole in less than a hunner years."

It was Father who gave us first a love for books, and taught us the magic of lovely words. And it was Father who tried to place our stumbling little childish feet in the Narrow Way, and to turn our eyes ever towards a better country—" that is an heavenly ! " I suppose it was the dimly-

understood talk of the better country that gave
John and me the idea of our Kingdom.

It was a great secret once, but now I may tell
without breaking faith   Boggley and the Bird were
prosaic people, caring more for bird-nesting and
Red Indian hunting than games of make-believe,
so they never knew.   It was part of the sunny old
garden, our Kingdom, and was called Nontland
because it was ruled by one Nont.   He had once
been a common ninepin, but having had a hole
bored through his middle with a red-hot wire he
became possessed of a mystic power and personality.
Even we—his creators, so to speak—stood somewhat in awe of him.

The River Beulah flowed through Nontland,
and it was bounded on the north by the Celestial
Mountains ; on the south by the red brick wall,
where the big pears grew ; on the west by the Rose
of Sharon tree ; and on the east by the pig-sty.
That last sounds something of a descent, but it
wasn't really a pig-sty, and I can't think why it
was called so, for, to my knowledge, it had never
harboured anything but two innocent white Russian
rabbits with pink eyes.   It was situated at the foot
of the kitchen-garden, next door to the hen-houses ;
the roof, made of pavement flags, was easy to

climb, and, sloping as it did to the top of the wall overlooking the high-road, was greatly prized by us as a watch-tower from which we could see the world go by.

To get into our Kingdom we knocked at the Wicket Gate, murmuring as we did so :

" El Dorado
Yo he trovado,"

and it opened—with a push   We hadn't an idea then, nor have I now, what the words meant. We got them out of a book called *The Spanish Brothers*, and thought them splendidly mysterious.

Besides ourselves, and Nont, and the Russian rabbits, there was only one other denizen of our Kingdom—a turkey with a broken leg, a lonely, lovable fowl which John, out of pity, raised to the peerage and the office of Prime Minister   I have a vivid recollection of riding in hot haste on a rake to tell the King—not in proper fairy fashion that the skies were fallen, but that Lord Turkey of Henhouse was dead.

John, I remember, always carried some fern seed in his trouser-pocket. He said it made him invisible—a delusion I loyally supported   It seems to me the sun always shone in those days, the time

was ever three o'clock in the afternoon, and they
lay just adown the road !

It has just occurred to me, and it is an awesome
thought, that you must converse every day, and
all day, in the German language. I believe I have
forgotten all I ever knew of German, though it
isn't so very long ago since I wrestled in tears and
confused darkness of mind with that uncouth tongue.
Don't forget your native tongue, and don't dare
write me a letter in German, or, like the Editor of
The Spectator, I shall say, " This correspondence
must now cease ! "

Since last I wrote life has been one long changing
of garments and moving from one show to another.
Tuesday was Viceroy's Cup Day at the races, a
very pretty sight. One side of the ground was
crowded by pretty women in lovely gowns, and on
the other side the natives sat in their hundreds and
chattered, not the drab-coloured crowd we produce,
but gay and striking as a bed of tulips.

There are three stands—one for the members of
the Turf Club, one for the ordinary public, and one
for the natives who can afford a seat. The members
of the Turf Club may be said to be the sheep ; the
others the goats. It is more comfortable in every
way to be a sheep. You get a better seat and a

comfortable tea in an enclosure, with the sight of
the goats scrambling wildly for a little refreshment
to keep you thankful, for in the heat and dust and
glare even a sheep is apt to lose sight of its mercies.
I thought G. was the prettiest girl there. She is
always such a refreshing sight, pink and white and
golden like a morning in May, and tall—"like a
king's own daughter."

I was with the Ormondes and, of course, Boggley.
Mrs. Ormonde is so charming, she is a great favourite
with men, and is always surrounded when she goes
anywhere by about half a dozen eager for her
smiles. She has the quaintest way of handing her
surplus cavaliers on to me, but I really much prefer
Victor and Boggley as companions They don't
need to be amused like other men, and are always
good-natured and funny.

I am feeling a little pale with all the excitement,
and shall be glad of the change to Darjeeling to-
morrow Next mail you shall hear all about it
—that is to say, if no person, seditiously inclined,
derails the train or does anything horrid. Some
very dreadful things have been happening lately,
but I don t think there is much danger so long as
we keep far from the vicinity of dignitaries.

7

Calcutta, New Year's Day.

WEDNESDAY already, the mail goes to-morrow, and I with so much to write about.

To begin—we left Calcutta on Friday afternoon and got to the Ganges about eight, when we embarked in a ferry-boat to cross the river It was quite a big steamer, with dinner-tables laid out on deck, decorated for Christmas with palm-branches, Chinese lanterns, and large, deadly-looking iced cakes.

On the other side, the train was waiting that was to take us to Siliguri, and we lost no time in looking for places. Indian trains are rather different from our trains. Each carriage has two broad seats running lengthways, which pull out for sleeping berths, and two other berths that let down from the roof. I found I had to share a carriage with two other females, and an upper berth fell to my share.

The bearer arranged my bed, and Boggley took a glance round, asked if I were all right, and departed to his own place. Isn't it a queer idea to carry one's bedding about with one? Pillows, blankets, and a quilt, all done up in a canvas hold-all, accompany people wherever they travel—in trains, hotels, even when staying with friends.

Well, there was I shut up for the night with two strange women, mother and daughter evidently, American certainly, and the horror of an upper berth staring me in the face ! It is quite an experience to sleep in the upper berth of an Indian train. To begin with, it takes an acrobat of no mean order to reach it at all, and once you are in your nose almost touches the roof of the carriage. As I climbed to my lofty perch one of the American ladies remarked, " I guess, child, you ain't going to have the time of your life up there to-night." And I hadn't. Every time the train gave a jolt—which it did every few seconds—I clung wildly to the straps to keep myself from descending suddenly and violently to the floor ; and in less than an hour every bone in my body was crying out against the inhuman hardness of my couch. In spite of everything, I fell asleep, and awoke feeling colder than I ever remember feeling before. I started up, banging my head on the roof as I did so, to find that the carriage door was swinging wide open. What was to be done ? I carefully felt the bumps beginning to rise on my forehead, and considered. It was, humanly speaking, impossible that I could descend and shut that door, and yet, could I endure lying inadequately covered and exposed to all the winds

of heaven ? There remained my fellow-travellers—
they at least were on the first floor, so to speak ;
but as I wavered a striking apparition rose, stalked
down the carriage, and, leaning far out into the
night, seized the door and shut it with a bang.
Then arose a shrill protest from beneath me :
" Oh, Mommer, how could you be so careless !
You might have fallen out, and I should have been
left quite alone in this awful heathen country ! "

After that there was no more sleep, and when
daylight came filtering through the shutters I slid
warily to the floor, and having washed and dressed,
sat on my dressing-bag and conversed amiably
with the Americans. I found them charming
and most entertaining, simple, quiet people ; not
the shrill-voiced tourist *jāt* at all. They had been
travelling, so they told me, with a sort of dreary
satisfaction, for two years, and they had still about
a year to do. It sounded like hard labour ! The
poor dears ! I can't think why they did it. They
would have been so much happier at home in their
own little corner of the world. I can picture them
attending sewing bees, and other quaint things people
do attend in old-fashioned New England story-
books. They had a servant with them whom they
addressed as Ali, a bearded rascal who evidently

cheated them at every turn, and who actually came
into their presence with his shoes on !

I didn't know till I met these Americans that I
was such a wit—or perhaps wag is a better word.
I didn't try to be funny, I didn't even know I was
being funny, but every word I said convulsed them.

The " Mommer " said to me :

" Child, are you married ? "

" No," I said, surprised.   " Why ? "

" I was just thinking what a good time your
husband must have ! "

When we reached Siliguri I was surprised to find
everything glistening with frost, and the few natives
who were about had their heads wrapped up in
shawls as if they were suffering from toothache.
We got some breakfast in the waiting-room, and
then took our places in the funniest little toy train.
This is the Darjeeling-Himalaya Railway   It was
all very primitive.   A man banged with a stick on
a piece of metal by way of a starting-bell, and we set
off on our journey to cloudland.

Eagerly looked for, Darjeeling came at last, but
alack ! no mountains, only piled-up banks of white
clouds.   It was bitterly cold, and we were glad to
get out and stamp up to the hotel, where we found
great fires burning in our rooms

There wasn't much to do in the hotel beyond reading back numbers of *The Lady's Pictorial*, and I went to bed on Saturday night rather low in my mind, fearing, after all, I was not to be accounted worthy to behold the mountains.

Some of the people in the hotel were getting up at 3.30 to go to Tiger Hill to see the sun rise on Everest. Boggley, the lazy one, wouldn't hear of going, and when I awoke in the grey dawning stiff with cold, in spite of a fire and heaps of blankets and rugs, I felt thankful that I hadn't a strenuous brother. If it had been John, I dare not think where he would have made me accompany him to in his efforts to get as near as possible to his beloved mountains. Never shall I forget the first time he took me to Switzerland to climb. I had never climbed before—unless you call scrambling on the hills at home climbing—and I was all eagerness to try till John gave me Whymper's book on Zermatt to amuse me in the train, and I read of the first ascent of the Matterhorn and its tragic sequel It had the effect of reducing me to a state of abject terror. All through that journey, from Paris to Lausanne, from Lausanne to Visp, from Visp to Zermatt, horror of the Matterhorn hung over me like a pall I even found something sinister in little Zermatt when we got there—Zermatt that now I love so, with the rushing, icy river, the cheerful smell of wood smoke, the goats that in the early morning wake one with the tinkle-tinkle of the bells through the street, and the quiet-eyed guides that sit on the wall in the twilight and smoke the pipe of peace.

After dinner, that first night, we walked through the village and along the winding path that leads up to the Schwarzsee, and gazed at the mighty peak, so wild, so savage in the pale purple light that follows the sunset glow—gazed at it in silence, John wrapped in adoration, I thinking of the men who had gone up this road to their death.

"Yes," said John, as we turned back, "some very scared men have come down this road"

If he had known what an exceedingly scared girl was at his side he wouldn't, I think, have chosen that moment to turn into the little graveyard that surrounds the village chapel, to look at the graves of the victims—the graves of Croz the guide, of Hudson, and the boy Hadow. The text on one stone caught my eye—"*Be ye therefore also ready* . . ." It was too much ; I fled back to the hotel, locked the door of my room, shuttered the

windows so that I should not see the vestige of a
mountain—and wept.

It is odd to think how I hated it all that night,
how to myself I maligned all climbers, calling them
in my haste foolhardy—senseless—imbecile, when I
had only to go up my first easy mountain to become
as keen as the worst—or the best.

Sometimes in those mountaineering excursions
with John to Zermatt, to Chamonix, to Grindelwald,
I have found it in my heart to envy the unaspiring
people who spend long days pottering about on
level ground   But looking back it isn't the quiet,
lazy days one likes to think about.   No—rather it
is the mornings when one rose at 2 a.m and, thrust-
ing aching feet into nailed boots, tiptoed noisily
into the deserted dining-room to be supplied with
coffee and rolls by a pitifully sleepy waiter.

Outside the guides wait, Joseph and Aloys, and
away we tramp in single file along the little path
that runs through fields full of wild flowers, drenched
with dew, into a fairy-tale wood of tall, straight
pine-trees. We follow the steady, slow footsteps
of Joseph, the chief guide, up the winding path that
turns and twists, and turns again, but rises, always
rises, until we are clear of the wood, past the rough,
stony ground, and on to the snow, firm and hard

to the feet before the sun has melted the night's
frost. When we reach the rocks, and before we
rope, Aloys removes his rucksack and proceeds to
lay out our luncheon; for if one breakfasts at two
one is ready for the next meal at nine. Crouched
in strange attitudes, we munch cold chicken, rolls
and hard-boiled eggs, sweet biscuits and apples,
with great content. Joseph has buried a bottle of
white wine in the snow, and now pours some into
a horn tumbler, which he hands to Mademoiselle
with an air—a draught of nectar. It is John's
turn for the tumbler next, and as he emerges from
the long, ice-cold, satisfying drink he declares
his firm intention, his unalterable resolve, never
to drink anything but white wine again in this
world. But doubtless as you know, the white wine
of the Lowlands is not the white wine of the mountains It needs to be buried in the snow by Joseph,
and drunk out of a horn tumbler, at the foot of an
aiguille, after a six hours' climb, to be at its best.
After refreshment comes the hard work To look
at the face of the rock up which Joseph has swarmed;
to say hopelessly, " I can't do it, I can't," and then
gradually to find here a niche for one hand, here a
foothold; to learn to cling to the rock, to use every
bit of oneself, to work one's way up delicately as a

cat so as not to send loose stones down on the
climber below, until, panting, one lands on the
ledge appointed by Joseph, there to rest while
the next man climbs, it is the best of sports. And
at the top to stand in the " stainless eminence of
air," to look down eight—ten—a thousand feet
to the toy village at the foot while John names
all the other angel peaks that soar round us, tell
me, you who are also a climber, is it not very
good ?

But the coming down ! Stumbling wearily down
the steep paths of the pine-woods with the skin
rubbed off one's toes, and giving at the knees like
an old and feeble horse, that is not so good. And
yet—I don't know. For as we near the valley,
puffs of hot, scented air come up to meet us, the
tinkle of the cow-bell greets our ears, and we realize
that it is only given to those who have braved the
perils, who have searched for the deep things of
the ancient mountains and found out the precious
things of the lasting hills, to thoroughly appreciate
the pleasant, homely quietness of the meadow-
lands.

But I have wandered miles away from Sunday
morning in Darjeeling.

It was still misty when we went out after break-

fast, but not so solidly misty, so Boggley held out
hopes it would clear.

Darjeeling is a pretty place tucked into the
mountain-side In the middle is the bazaar, and
it happened to be market day, which made it more
interesting. The village street was lined on both
sides with open booths, some piled with fruit and
vegetables; others, oddly enough, with lamps and
mirrors and other cheap rubbish which bore the
legend " Made in Germany," others with 'all sorts
of curios The place was thronged with people. A
few plainsmen and Tibetans Boggley pointed out,
but most of the crowd were hill-people, jolly little
squat men and women hung with silver chains and
heavy ear-rings set with turquoises. Their eyes
are very black and all puckered with laughing,
and they have actually rosy cheeks.

They crowded round, trying to sell us curios and
lumps of rough turquoise When we asked the
price of anything, they replied promptly, " Twenty
rupees." We would offer two rupees, and, after
a few minutes' bargaining, they took it quite
cheerfully, the thing probably not being worth
eight annas. I bought a prayer-wheel It is a
round silver thing with a handle rather like a
child's rattle, and inside are slips of paper covered

with writing. These are the prayers, and at
intervals you twirl the wheel round, and the oftener
you turn it the more devout you are

I also purchased some lumps of rough turquoise,
though Boggley said they were not a good blue,—
too pale,—and was tying them up in my handker-
chief when Boggley gripped my arm. "Look!"
he said. I looked straight across the valley.
"Higher," said Boggley, and I lifted my eyes
literally' to the skies; and there—"suddenly—
behold—beyond"—were the everlasting snows.

All day they stayed with us, and as the sun was
setting we climbed to a point of vantage to see the
last of them. It has been said they are a snow-
white wall barring the whole horizon They are
like a city carved by giants out of eternal ice, a
city which lieth four-square. We watched while
peak after peak faded into cold greyness: until
Kangchenjunga towered, alone, rose-red into the
heavens, sublime in its "valorous isolation." Then
the light left it too, and we turned and came down
from the Hill of God.

We left for Calcutta at noon on Monday, and I
had a thoroughly over-eaten, uncomfortable day,
all owing to Boggley's forethought. He said as we
began breakfast about nine o'clock : "Now eat a

good breakfast, for we shall have to leave before lunch, and no man knows when we shall get another meal."

It seemed good common-sense, so I ate an egg and two pieces of toast after I had really finished. That was all very well, but the hotel people thoughtfully provided us with a substantial luncheon before we left. Even then Boggley kept on looking to the future.

"Oh, tuck in," he said. "We shan't get anything more till eight o'clock."

I didn't feel as if I wanted anything ever again, but I hurriedly gobbled some food, and we raced to the station, then sat in the train half an hour before it started

At the first station we stopped at, the bearer appeared at the carriage window with a breakfast cup of tea and a large " y-sponge-cake," ferreted from no man knows where. He was so pleased with himself that I hadn't the heart to refuse it— so there were three meals that ought to have been spread over the greater part of the day crowded into one morning. I sympathized with the vulture, who

" Eats between his meals,
    And that's the reason why
He very, very rarely feels
    As well as you and I."

It is never pleasant to come down from the heights, and we had rather a dreary journey to Siliguri.

Boggley had taken care to wire for a lower berth in the train for me, but it seems ordained that I shall ascend in Indian trains. I again found myself in a carriage with my Americans, and the daughter had such bad toothache, and seemed so much to dread the prospect of mounting to the eyrie, that I had to say that I would rather like it for myself.

Toothache kept Miss America awake and made her talkative, which was unfortunate for me. She wanted to know all about the manners and customs of the British. She only knew us from the outside, so to speak. Incidentally she shed a lurid light on the habits of the American male. It seems that young men in America are expected to carry offerings of fruit and flowers and candy to young women—not when they are engaged, mark you ; what is expected of them then I daren't think—but to quite irrelevant young women. "Don't young gentlemen do so in England ? " asked Miss America. "No," I said, feeling that I was making out my countrymen poor, mean creatures indeed, but feeling also how much more

complicated life would become for these "gentlemen of England now abed" if they had to carry
crates of oranges, drums of figs, and pounds of
candies to every casual young woman whose
acquaintance they enjoyed.

"You don't say!" said Miss America. "And
don't they take you out driving in their buggies?"

"*Never*," I replied firmly. "They haven't got
them."

"You don't say! And how does a young
gentleman show he admires you?"

"Well, he doesn't as a rule," I murmured feebly.

"I guess," she said, "we manage things better
in America." And, indeed, perhaps they do.

This conversation so exhausted us that we fell
very sound asleep, and knew nothing till we arrived
at the station where we had to get out and change
into the ferry-boat. Then there was a terrible
scurry. The servants waiting to pack up the
bedding and strap bags—they said they had
wakened us at the previous station, but they must
have wakened someone else instead—while we
threw on various articles of clothing, stuck hats on
undone hair, and feet into unlaced shoes, all the
while, like a Greek chorus, the "Mommer" moaning reproachfully, "Oh, Ali, you might have woke

us," while outside on the platform bounded the irate Boggley speaking wingèd words.

We did get on to the boat, so after all there was no harm done.

I was quite sorry to part with my Americans when we reached Calcutta They and their Ali were going on to Benares that night, tired and spiritless. They shook us both violently by the hand, vowing we were just "lovely people" and that I was a "real little John Bull!"

The home mail was waiting us when we got back, and I read my letters, slept for an hour or two, and then got up and went to a big New Year's dinner-party, where we had fireworks in our crackers, and sang what G. calls "Oldlangzine."

Thanks so much for your delightfully long letter. My wrist aches so I can't write another word.

Calcutta, Jan. 8.

ONE more week and we start for the Mofussil and the Simple Life. The Mofussil, I may remark in passing, is not, as at first I thought, some sort of prophet, but means simply the country districts.

I have been standing over Bella while she laid out all my dresses, telling her which are to be packed carefully and left in Calcutta, and which are to accompany me. I don't want to take any more luggage than I can help, as it is, I foresee we shall have a mountain Boggley has been begging everyone for the loan of books, as he does not see how I am to be kept in reading matter when there are no libraries within reach. He accuses me of being capable of finishing two fat volumes in a day, but I shan't have time to read much if I carry out my great project. *I am going to write a book.* You are surprised ? But why ? Other members of the family can write, why not I ? I read in a review lately that John has great distinction of style, so perhaps I have too. Anyway, I have bought a pile of essay-paper and sixpenny-worth of J nibs, and I mean to find out. It is to be a book about the Mutiny, the information to be derived from Trevelyan's book on Cawnpore There is room, don't you think, for a really good book on the Mutiny ?

Last night the Drawing-Room was held by the Vicereine, a function that everyone, more or less, is expected to attend. I went with G. and her sister (one needn't go with the lady who presents

8

one), and found it most entertaining. Not being
the wives or daughters of Members of Council or
anything *burra*, we hadn't the private entrée, and
had to wait our turn in pens, like dumb driven
cattle.

It is a much simpler affair than a presentation
at home ; one need not even wear veils and feathers,
and the trains of our white satin gowns were modest
as to length. It was silly to be nervous about
such a little thing, but I quite shook with terror.
I think it was the being passed along by A.D.C.'s
that unnerved me, but when I reached the last
and heard " To be presented," and my name
shouted out, I stotted (do you know the Scots word
to stot ? It means to walk blindly—to stumble
—that and much more ; oh ! a very expressive
word) over a length of red carpet that seemed to
stretch for miles, feeling exactly as a Dutch wooden
doll looks ; saw, as in a glass darkly, familiar faces
that smiled jeeringly, or encouragingly, I could
not be sure which ; ducked feebly and uncertainly
before the two centre figures ; and, gasping relief,
found myself going out of the doorway walking
on G.'s train.

Afterwards, when we were all gathered upstairs,
the many pretty gowns and uniforms made a gay

sight. I saw the dearest little Maharanee blazing
in magnificent jewels and looking so scared, and
shy, and sweet. There was a supper-room, and
lots to eat if one could have got at it, or had had
room to eat it after it had been got. I don't like
champagne—" simpkin " they call it here—much
to drink, but I like it less when it is shot down my
back by a careless man

There is a fancy-dress ball to-night at Government House, and that is the last of my dissipations
for some time to come.

I go on writing, writing all the time about my
own affairs and never even mention your letters, and
nothing makes me so cross as to have people do
that to me. I like my friends to make interested
comments on everything I tell them

I am glad you are so happy in your work and
enjoy life. Is the book nearly finished yet? It is
nice that you have found such charming friends
Is the Fräulein person you talk about pretty? I
can imagine how you enjoy hearing her play and
singing to her accompaniment   I always think of
you when I hear good music, and of your face when
I told you that the only music I really liked was
Scots songs played on the pianola ! But you know
that is really true. I simply hate good music.

Once, in Paris, I went with some people to hear
Samson et Delilah, and while everyone sat rapt,
enchanted by the sweet sounds, I waited with
what patience I could till the stage temple fell,
in the vain hope that some part would hit the
tenor. What would your Fräulein say to such
blasphemy?

Forgive me maligning the gods of your idolatry
I think I had better finish this letter before I go
on from bad to worse, because I am in an unaccount-
ably perverse and impertinent frame of mind to-day,
and there is no saying what I shall say next.

Calcutta, Jan. 8

Such a scene of confusion! Everything I possess
is lying on the floor. All the things I have accumu-
lated on my way out and since I came to Calcutta
lie in one heap waiting to be packed, shoes, dresses,
hats, books, photographs are scattered madly about,
and in the middle, almost reduced to idiocy, and
making no effort to reduce chaos to order, sits
Bella I can't help her, for I must get my home
letters written and posted before we leave Calcutta,

for before I reach my first halting-place the mail
will be gone.

Boggley has been in the Mofussil for three days,
and I have been staying with the Townleys. I
came back last night. It was nice being with G
again, and her sister is extraordinarily kind. We
had rather an interesting day on Friday. I have
always been asking where are the Missionaries, but
I suppose I must have asked the wrong people, for
they didn't seem to know. However, the other
day I met a lady,—Mrs Gardner,—the wife of a
missionary, who asked us to go to lunch with her,
and promised she would show us something of the
work among the women. So on Friday we set off
in a *tikka-gharry*.

We left the Calcutta we knew—the European
shops, the big, cool houses, the Maidan—and drove
through native streets, airless, treeless, drab-coloured
places, until we despaired of ever reaching anywhere
When at last our man did stop, we found Mrs.
Gardner's cool, English-looking drawing-room a
welcome refuge from the glare and the dust ; and
she was kindness itself. She made a delightful
cicerone, for she has a keen sense of humour and a
wide knowledge of native life.

We went first to see the girls' school—a quaint

sight. All the funny little women with their hair
well oiled and plastered down, with iron bangles
on their wrists to show that they were married,
wrapped in their *saris*, so demurely chanting their
lessons! When we went in they all stood up and,
touching their foreheads, said in a queer sing-song
drawl, "Salaam, Mees Sahib, salaam!" The teachers
were native Bible-women. The schoolrooms opened
on to a court with a well like a village pump in the
middle. ' One small girl was brought out to tell
us the story of the Prodigal Son in Bengali, which
she did at great length with dramatic gestures ;
but our attention was somewhat diverted from her
by a small boy who ran in from the street, hot and
dusty, sluiced himself unconcernedly all over at the
pump, and raced out again dripping. It did look
so inviting.

When we left the school Mrs. Gardner said she
would take us to see some *purdah nashin* women—
that is, women who never go out with their faces
uncovered, and who never see any men but their
own husbands.

I don't quite know what we expected to see—
something very Oriental and luxurious anyhow ;
marble halls and women with veils and scarlet
satin trousers dotted about on cushions—and the

reality was disappointing. No marble halls, no
divans and richly carved tables, no hookahs and
languid odours of rich perfumes, but a room with
cheap modern furniture, china ornaments, and a
round table in the middle of the floor, for all the
world like the best parlour of the working classes.
Two women lived there with their husbands and
families, and they came in and looked G. and me all
over, fingered our dresses, examined our hats, and
then asked why we weren't married ! I could see
they didn't like the look of us at all. They said we
were like the dolls their little girls got at the fête,
and produced two glassy-eyed atrocities with flaxen
hair and vivid pink cheeks, and asked if we saw the
resemblance. We didn't. They told Mrs. Gardner
—who has been many years in India, and looks it—
that they thought she was much nicer-looking than
we were, her face was all one colour ! (They
spoke, of course, in Bengali, but Mrs Gardner trans-
lated.) Poor women ! what a pitifully dull life is
theirs ! G. was disappointed to hear they hadn't
become Christians. She had an idea that the Missionary had only to appear with the Gospel story
and the deed was done. I'm afraid it isn't as easy
as that by a long way.

Mrs. Gardner read a chapter from the Bible while

we were there, and these women argued with her
most intelligently. They are by no means stupid.
Before we left G sang to them, with no accompaniment but a cold stare. When she finished they said
they preferred Bengali music, it had more tune
We left, feeling we had been no success

Having seen a comparatively well-to-do household, Mrs. Gardner said she would show us a really
poor one We followed her through a network of
lanes more evil-smelling than anything I ever imagined—London can't compete with Calcutta in
the way of odours—until we reached a little hovel
with nothing in it but a string-bed, a few cooking-
pots, and two women Caste, it seems, has nothing
to do with money, and these women, though as poor
as it is possible to be, were thrice-born Brahmins,
and received us with the most gracious, charming
manners, inviting us to sit on the string-bed w ile
they stood before us with meekly folded hands. The
dim interior of the hut with its sun-bleached mud
floor, the two gentle brown-eyed women with their
saris and silver anklets, looking wonderingly at G.
in her white dress sitting enthroned, with her blue
eyes shining and her hair a halo, made an unforget-
table picture of the East and the West

We had tea at the Mission House and met several

missionary ladies who told us much that was interesting about their work, which they seem to love whole-
heartedly. I asked one girl how it compared with
work among the poor at home, and she said, " Well,
perhaps it is the sunshine, but here it is never
sordid." I can't agree. To me the eternal sunshine
makes it worse   At home, although the poverty
and misery are terrible, still, I comfort myself, the
poor have their cosy moments. In winter sometimes, when funds run to a decent fire and a kippered herring to make a savoury smell, a brown
teapot on the hob and the children gathered in,
they are as happy as possible for the time being ;
I have seen them. I can't imagine any brightness
in the lives of the women we saw.

To be a missionary in Calcutta, I think one would
require to have an acute sense of humour and no
sense of smell. Am I flippant ? I don't mean to
be, because I feel I can't sufficiently admire the men
and women who are bearing the heat and burden of
the day. And now that sounds patronizing, and
Heaven knows I don't mean to be that.

Anyway, G. and I were never intended to be missionaries. We drove home very silent, in the only
vehicle procurable, a third-class *tikka-gharry*, feeling as if all the varied smells of the East were lying

heavy on our chests. Once G. said gloomily.
" How long does typhoid fever take to come out ? "
which made me laugh weakly most of the way home.

13th.

THE day of our departure has come, and Boggley
is behaving dreadfully. Having taken time by the
forelock, I am packed and ready, but Boggley has
done nothing He remarked airily that I must go
to the Stores and get some sheets, a new mosquito-
net, and a supply of pots and pans, and then went
off to lunch with someone at the Club, leaving me
speechless with rage. How can I possibly know
what sort of pots and pans are wanted ? I never
camped out before. I shall calmly finish this letter
and pay no attention to his order.

We had a farewell dinner last night, the Ormondes
and one or two others. We came into this dis-
mantled room afterwards and talked till midnight,
and amused ourselves vastly. I happened to say
that I was rather scared at the thought of the wild
beasts I might encounter, probably under my camp-
bed, in the jungle ; so a man, Captain Rawson, drew
out a table for me to take with me into camp. One
heave and a wriggle means a boa-constrictor, two

heaves and a growl a tiger—and so on. So you can imagine me in a tent, in the dead of night, sitting up, anxiously striking matches and consulting my table as to what is attacking me.

Mrs. Ormonde, who is so nervous that if a cracker goes off in her hearing she thinks it is another Mutiny, is anxious that we should take guns with us into the Mofussil in case we are attacked. Picture to yourself Boggley and me setting out " with a little hoard of Maxims." Armed, I should be a menace alike to friend and foe !

My first stopping-place is Takai. Boggley is going to some very far-away place where it wouldn't be convenient to take a female, so when Dr. and Mrs. Russel asked me to come to them while he is there I very gladly accepted the invitation. Dr. Russel is a medical missionary. I don't know him, but his wife, a very clever, interesting woman, I met when she was last home, and she told me about her home in the jungle until I longed to see it. Boggley will come for me in about ten days. Bella I shall leave in Calcutta. It would be a nuisance carting her about from place to place, and I am not so helpless that I can't manage for myself.

Expect next mail to receive a budget of pro-digious size.

THE SUNBURNED EARTH

Takai, Jan. 19.

THERE is no doubt this is the ideal place for letter-writing. I sit here, in the verandah, with long, quiet hours stretching out before me and nothing to do but write and write, and I suppose that is why for the last thirty minutes I have sat nibbling the end of my pen and dreaming—without putting pen to paper.

Where did I leave off? The Monday we left Calcutta, wasn't it? To continue. The said Monday was a strenuous day. Boggley absented himself till late afternoon, while I wrestled with wild beasts at Ephesus in the shape of bearers and coolies, my Hindustani deserting me utterly, as it always does at a crisis. G., desolated at the thought of the coming separation, hovered round all day and did her best to help.

About tea-time Boggley walked in, serenely regardless of the fact that we were still devoid of bed and table linen, crockery and cooking utensils. In the end the bearer was dispatched to the Stores with a list, but the result of his shopping I haven't yet seen. G. stayed till nearly dinner-time, and sang to us for a last time   It was horrid parting from her, my dear old G.   Do I write too much about her ?   I thought from something you said in a letter that perhaps I rather bored you talking of her.   You see, I like her so much, and you can hardly understand how much she has meant to me since we left England together that showery October day.

After dinner we said good-bye to our friends in what Boggley irreverently calls " the hash-house," and at nine o'clock departed to the station.   The bearer was there with all the luggage, and the *syces* with the ponies, for we are taking the ponies in case there is a chance of polo.   In the end we nearly missed the train.   At the booking-office, when we tried to book the ponies, the babu in charge lost his presence of mind and turned round and round like a teetotum   I was amazed at Boggley's patience.   For myself, I was conscious of an intense, and most unladylike, desire to slap the poor babu I, who have constantly protested against any want of consideration in the treatment of natives !

As I was the only lady travelling, the guard was much against giving me a carriage to myself, but a man who spoke with authority, hearing us argue,

came up and told him to put a "Ladies Only"
placard on my carriage, so I travelled in lonely
splendour.

At Assansol, which we reached at 5 a.m., we had
chota-hazri. Tea and toast, and most diminutive
eggs, which we had to hold in our fingers as there
were no egg-cups.

Simultala was my destination, and about eleven
o'clock we reached it. Underneath the trees a few
yards away from the little station we found a bullock-
cart, which the Russels had sent for my luggage, and
a doolie for myself   A doolie is a kind of string-bed
hung on a pole, with a covering to keep off the sun.
It is carried by four men, and two others run alongside to relieve their companions at intervals.   I
had sixteen miles to travel in this thing.   I looked
at Boggley very doubtfully, and he tried to en-
courage me.

"It is really quite comfortable," he said (and
when he said so he lied), "and the men go very fast
You will be there in no time."   So I bundled in
somehow, said a wistful good-bye to Boggley, and
we started   I can't honestly say I like a doolie
I would rather have been my luggage and gone in
the bullock-cart.   Whichever way I lay I very soon
got an ache in my back.   The conduct, too, of the

9

coolies filled me with uneasiness They kept up a
continued groaning One said, " Oh--oh—oh ! "
and the other replied, " Oo—oo—oo ! " and you can't
think what a depressing sound it was (I know now
that doolie-coolies always make that noise when
on duty. It seems to keep up their hearts, so to
speak, and cheer them on) Feeling guiltily that it
was my weight that made them groan, I lay perfectly still, and was even holding my breath in an
effort to make myself lighter, when, for no apparent
reason, we left the road, such as it was, and started
across the trackless plain. There was nothing to be
seen except an infrequent bush, no trace of a human
habitation—nothing but the wind blowing and the
grass growing. Awful thoughts began to come into
my head. I was all alone in India, indeed worse
than alone, I was in the company of six natives
most inadequately clothed : of their language I
knew not one single word ; I didn't even know if
they were carrying me in the direction I wanted
to go. Suddenly the groaning ceased, and I found
myself and the doolie planted on the ground. *Was
my bright young life to be ended ?* Cold with terror,
I shut my eyes tight, and when I opened them I
found all the six coolies squatted round, all talking
at once, all presumably addressing me. I made

out one word which was repeated often, *baksheesh*. Reminding myself that I was of the Dominant Race, I sat up and waving a hand towards the horizon said sternly, " Jao ! " I do think I must have intimidated them, for they meekly picked me up again and we resumed our journey. The longest lane turns, the darkest night wears on to dawn, the weariest river winds at last to the sea , and about tea-time, aching, dishevelled, hungry (having had nothing but a few chocolates since *chotā-hazri* at 5 a.m.), I was deposited before the verandah of the Russels' bungalow.

I don't suppose you know anything about mission work ? Neither do I, which is very shocking, as I have had every opportunity of acquiring information. Perhaps, as a child, I was taken to too many missionary meetings, with their atmosphere of hot tea and sentiment, and heard *too* much of " my dear brothers and sisters in the mission field," for I grieve to say, before I came to India, I quite actively disliked missionaries and thought them a feeble folk. Mother was the only kind of missionary I liked   She has a mission—so we tell her— to the dreary people of this world. Not the very poor—they are vastly entertaining—but the not-very-rich, highly respectable, deadly dull people,

with awkward, unlovable manners, whom no one
cares very much to visit or to ask to things, and
who must often feel very lonely and neglected.
While others are taken up with more entertaining
company Mother has time to trot to these people
with a new book or magazine, or merely to talk for
half an hour in the funny bright way which is like
no one else's way, has them to the house to meet
interesting people (in spite of the remonstrant groans
of the family), and having brought them does not
neglect them, but draws them out till they seem
quite brilliant, and they go away warmed and
enlivened by their social success.

Even the most determined distruster of missions
couldn't stay long at Takai without being con-
verted Dr. Russel, very far from being feeble, is
a most able man, who would have made his mark
in his profession at home ; but he prefers healing the
bodies and saving the souls of the Santals in the
jungle, to building up a lucrative practice, and even
attaining the dizzy height of a knighthood.

To heal their poor neglected bodies ; to be the
first to tell them of Jesus—how did Festus put it ?—
" one Jesus, which is dead, whom Paul affirmed
to be alive " ; to teach them, to help and raise
them until life becomes for these natives a new and

undreamed-of thing—one can see how fine it is,
how soul-satisfying !

Dr. Russel has built a hospital, and the natives
come from far and near bringing their sick. As I
sit here writing, they come trooping past, taking a
short cut past the bungalow, stopping to stare at
me quite unabashed, sometimes carrying a sick
child, sometimes a blind old man or woman. They
know they can come at any time and the Padre
Sahib will never tell them to go away. It is different
with a Government official He is hedged round
by *chuprassis* who levy toll on the poor natives
before they allow them to enter the presence of the
Sahib. It is a scandal, but it seems impossible to
stop it. You may catch a *chuprassi* in the act,
you may beat him and insist on his handing back
the money, but almost before your back is turned
the annas or pice have changed hands again ! It
is *dustoor* !

My first view of the hospital was rather a shock.
Nothing was what I had expected,. The beds are
square blocks of cement, without even a mattress.
The patients bring their own bedding and their
cooking pots and pans, and generally a friend to
look after them. The said friends camp all round
the hospital, and it is pretty to see them at sunset,

each cooking his evening meal over his own little
fire. This morning being Sunday I went to a service
at the hospital. The mingled smell of carbolic,
hookahs, and coco-nut oil was, I confess, rather
overpowering, but when Dr. Russel asked me, " Is
this at all interesting to you, or is it merely disgusting ? " I could reply truthfully that it was more
interesting than disgusting. The patients sat rolled
up in their blankets, and listened while the tale of
the Prodigal Son was read to them, holding up their
hands in horror when they heard he herded swine .
they regard that as a very low job indeed. It is odd
the way they respond : just as if during church
service at home a man were to answer each state-
ment made by the clergyman, " Right you are,
guv'nor."

Coming home, we saw a native cooking his dinner
on a little charcoal fire, and as I passed he threw
the contents of the pot away. Surprised, I asked
why. " Because," I was told, " your shadow fell
on it and defiled it ¹ "

One can hardly overestimate the boon a man
like Dr. Russel is to a district. Trust is a plant
of slow growth with the natives, but they have
learned to trust him entirely, and go to him in all
their troubles as children go to a father. And he

has a very real helpmate in his wife. I never saw
such a busy woman. If she isn't in the hospital
helping at operations (she has a medical degree),
she is teaching girls to sew, or women to read,
and yet the children are beautifully cared for, and
the house excellently managed. I suppose most
women would pity Mrs. Russel sincerely She
passes her life in a place many miles from another
European, with absolutely no society, no gaieties,
no theatres, not even shops where she can while
away the time buying things she doesn't want.
Yet I never met a woman so utterly satisfied with
her lot. Honestly, I don't think she has a single
thing left to wish for : devoted to her husband,
devoted to her children, heart and soul in her work

"If only," she sometimes says, " it would go on !
The children will have to go home very soon—the
tragedy of Anglo-Indian life."

They are such dear children, Ronald and Robert
and tiny Jean. The boys speak Santali like little
natives, and even their English has an odd turn.
When little Jean was born they were greatly interested in the first white baby they had seen, and
Ronald said rapturously :

"Oh, Mummy, aren't ladies darlings when they
are babies ? "

Their mother found them one day bending over the cradle, arguing as to why the baby cried

Ronald said, "She has no teeth, for that reason she cries."

Robert said, "She has no hair, for that reason she cries."

And Ronald finished, "She has no English, for that reason she cries."

I am not the only visitor at Takai. There are two missionary ladies here, resting after a strenuous time in some famine district. One is tall and stout, the other is short and thin ; both have drab-coloured faces and straight mouse-coloured hair ; both wear eye-glasses and sort of up and down dresses—the very best of women one feels sure, but oh ! so difficult. You know my weakness for making people like me, but these dear ladies will have none of me, charm I never so wisely. Everything I do meets with their disapproval—how well I see it in their averted, spectacled eyes! I talk too much, laugh too much, tell foolish tales, mimic my elders and betters, and—worst sin of all—I have never read, never even heard of, the *Missionary Magazine.*

Something you said in your last letter, some allusion to religion, I didn't quite like, and at any other time I would have written you a sermon

on the subject. In Calcutta (where I felt so self-
righteous) nothing would have prevented me—but
now I haven't the spirit   Mark, please, how the
whirligig of Time brings its revenges ! In Calcutta
I thought myself a saint, in Takai I am regarded
as a Brand Unplucked.   It is rather dispiriting   I
am beginning to wonder if I really am as nice as
I thought I was

Takai, Jan 22

THIS Gorgeous East is a cold and draughty place.

We have *chota-hazri* in the verandah at 7 30,
and at that early hour it is so cold my blue fingers
will hardly lift the cup. Now the sun is beginning
to warm things into life again, and I have been
sitting outside basking in its rays, to the anxiety
of Mrs. Russel, who, like all Anglo-Indians, has a
profound respect for the power of the Eastern sun.
The children are taught that one thing they must
not do is to run out without a topi   They were
looking over *The Pilgrim's Progress* with me, and
at a picture of Christian, bareheaded, approaching
the Celestial City, with the rays of the sun very
much in evidence, Robert pointed an accusing

finger, saying, " John Bunyan, you're in the sun without your topi."

The poor Santals must feel dreadfully cold just now, especially the children, who have hardly anything on. Mrs Russel has a big trunk full of things sent out from home as presents to the Mission—pieces of calico, and various kinds of garments—and these are given as prizes to the children who attend the Christian schools. The pieces of cloth which they can wind round them are the most valued prizes. Some of the garments are too ridiculous Shapeless sacks of pink flannelette, intended, I suppose, for shirts ; and such-like. This morning there was a prize-giving The big trunk was brought into the verandah, and the children were allowed to choose One small boy chose a dressing-gown of a material known, I believe, as duffle, of a striking pattern In this he arrayed himself with enormous pride · a wide frilled collar stood out round his little thin neck, and, to complete the picture, he carried a bow and arrow. A quainter figure I never saw ! I only wished the well-meaning Dorcas who made the garment could have seen him. A little missionary from somewhere in West Africa once told me about a small orphan native she had rescued and adopted

"I had him christened," she said plaintively. "I had him christened David Livingstone, and I dressed him in a blue serge man-of-war suit; but he ran away." I murmured sympathy, but I couldn't feel surprised. Imagine a little heathen David Livingstone, in a hot, sticky serge suit!

These bows and arrows, by the way, are rather interesting. The natives make them of bamboo and strips of hide, and they are tipped with iron. They really shoot things with them—birds and wild animals, I mean. I bought one from the owner of the dressing-gown for four annas, to take home to Peter. It seemed very little for a real bow and arrow, but Dr. Russel said it was quite enough; and when one comes to think of it, it is double a man's day's wage. I *am* enjoying myself at Takai. As the man said when he lost his wife, "It's verra quiet but verra peacefu'." After Calcutta, the quiet does seem almost uncanny

It is a blameless existence one leads. I think I would soon grow very good, for there is no temptation to be anything else   One can't be very frivolous when there is no one to be frivolous with; nor can one backbite and be unkind, for there is no provocation   As for being vain and fond of the putting on of apparel, what is the good when one is the Best People if one wears a garment of any description ?

Although there is nothing to do, the days never seem too long. After *chota-hazri* I generall go for a walk with the children There is one good broad road passing the bungalow which leads away to the Back of Beyond, but we prefer the little tracks worn by the feet of the natives, which criss-cross everywhere Jean won't stir a step without a horrid, dilapidated rag doll called Topsy. I do dislike the faces of rag dolls, their lack of profile is so gruesome, and Topsy is a most depressing speci-men of her kind ; but Jean lavishes affection on her. A woman-child is an odd thing. I remember being taken into a shop to choose a doll. and I chose a most hideous thing with curly white hair. No one could understand why, and I was too shy to tell. It was because the doll was so ugly , I felt sure no one would buy her, and I couldn't bear to think of her loneliness. The boys christened her " Mrs. Smilie," after a lady of that name whom they thought she resembled, and the poor thing came to a tragic end. They were playing at the execution of Mary Queen of Scots, in the shrubbery, seized on " Mrs. Smilie " to play the title rôle, and with brutal realism chopped off her poor ugly head. I arrived just in time to see the deed, and rushed swiftly, with fists and feet, to avenge her fate.

Well, we set off every morning on our pilgrimage, Jean calling herself "Mrs. Jones," and walking primly till we reach what we pretend is the sea-shore, where she forgets her dignity and rolls about in the sand   A certain kind of tree that Dr. Russel has planted round about the bungalow makes a noise exactly like waves, so it is easy to pretend about the sea. We meet many pilgrims on their way to some holy place, and we create quite a sensation in the little clusters of huts—they could hardly be called villages—that we pass through. The inhabitants crowd around us, saying " Johar," which I take it is Santali for " Salaam," and we repeat " Johar " and grin broadly in reply ; and the pie dogs sniff round us in a friendly way. The other day we met a boy who, on beholding me, stood stock still, threw back his head, and shouted with laughter. I never heard more whole-hearted merriment. I had to join in. Whether it was that he had never seen anyone with fair hair before, or whether there is something particularly droll in my appearance, I don't know, but he evidently found me the funniest thing he had met with for a long time. It is generally Topsy who is the centre

of interest. They hustle one another to look
at her and gurgle with delight. Jean told me
solemnly, " I have to leave her at home when I go
with Mummy to the villages. They won't listen
about Jesus for looking at Topsy."

Jean's great desire is to meet " someone white "
Yesterday I saw a horseman approaching in
European riding kit and a topi. " Look, Jean," I
said, " I believe that is an Englishman ; " but when
he came up to us and raised his topi with a flourish
Jean said mournfully, " No, it's nobody white,"
and I had to pick her up hurriedly in case she should
say something more to hurt the poor Eurasian.

When we come in from our walk it is tiffin-time.
After that the children are put to bed, and I sit
in the verandah and write and rest. Did I say
rest ?   This is what goes on :

" O-liv-i-a ! "

I go into the nursery, and Jean, very wide awake,
demands a needle and thread, as she wants to sew
a dress for Topsy.   I tie a piece of thread into a large
darning-needle and supply her with my handker-
chief, which she proceeds to sew into a tight ball.
I return to my writing

" Olivia ! "

This time it is Robert.

"Olivia, if this bungalow fell into the tank would it splash out all the water?"

"Of course it would."

"Then what would the water do when it fell back from the splash and found the bungalow blocking up its tank?"

Unable to think of an answer, I tell him to be a good boy and not disturb people when they are writing. Ronald begs for a piece of paper and a pencil, and having got it, proceeds to write down everything beginning with G   I once told Peter to do that, and his list when I looked at it ran : "God—Gollywog—Gordon Highlanders." . . .

Immediately I resume my writing it begins again, "Olivia" in every tone, peremptory, beseeching, coaxing—but like the deaf adder I stop my ears and refuse to hear.   I am using this opportunity to write my great work on the Mutiny, and it isn't nearly so easy to write a book as I thought No matter how much I try, my sentences seem all to stand up on end.   I can't acquire any ease or grace of style.   I read somewhere lately that young writers use too many adjectives, that good writers depend more on verbs   It has made me rather nervous and I keep counting both, but a certain dubiety in my own mind as to which is which greatly

complicates matters   My heroine, too, is a failure
I like her name—Belinda—but it is the only thing
I like about her.   What is the good of me laboriously
writing down that she is beautiful and charming
when I am convinced in my own mind she is nothing
of the kind ?   However, I mean to persevere . . .

We all meet at tea—the nicest time of the day
I think.   My friend Katie says the world isn't
properly warmed up till five o'clock. and certainly
there is a feeling of comfort all over everything
at the clink of the teacups   Mrs. Russel being
Scots, knows how to give a proper tea, with plates,
and knives, and scones, and jam ; and I am as
greedy as a schoolboy over it.   Yesterday there
was no milk—such a blow.   The cows had wandered
into a man's land, and he, as the custom is. marched
them into the pound five miles away, and there
we were—milkless !

The country round Takai is quite pretty—almost
like Scots moorland   Yesterday we went for a
picnic to a river at the opening of a pass—a most
interesting place where not very long ago a native
boy had been eaten by a tiger.   You see, picnics
in the jungle are not quite the insipid things they
are at home !   There is always the chance that the
unwary may be devoured.   Actually we did see

yesterday the footprints of a tiger in the sand by
the river—pugs I think is the proper expression.
I was scared, but Robert advanced boldly into the
bushes   Ronald, watching him admiringly, said,
"He is very brave ; he is as brave as Daniel "

Talking about tigers, they aren't nearly as pre-
valent as I thought. I had an idea they were
prowling all over India waiting to spring, but one
man told me he had been in India fifteen years
and had never seen one. Boggley came on one
once and took it for a cow—short-sighted Boggley !
Dr. Russel says there was a man-eating tiger in
the district lately, and a reward was offered for its
capture. A young engineer sallied forth to slay.
He directed the natives to dig a pit near where the
tiger was known to be and cover it with branches,
and the next day went and found it had walked
into the trap. The natives removed the branches,
the gallant engineer approached, but they had dug
the pit on a slope, and the tiger *came walking up to
meet him !*

I would rather like to see a wild beast from a
safe distance. A native came into hospital only
yesterday with his arm all torn and mauled by a
leopard, but, though I have walked miles through
the jungle, I have seen nothing more fearsome
10

than a black-beetle, and *that* I might have seen
at home. The Santals are very keen *shikaris,*
and go regularly to hunt armed with bows and
arrows and a few guns.

One morning I watched them start. With them
was a youth home on holiday from a situation in
Calcutta—I liked his idea of a shooting costume.
He wore a pair of bright blue socks and yellow
shoes, a pink shirt worn over a dhoti, and over
that a well-cut tweed coat (evidently an old one
of his master's), a high linen collar, but no tie, a
straw hat and enormous blue spectacles The last-
named were evidently worn more for effect than by
order of the oculist, for the youth removed them
when the time came to use his gun.

                                              27th.

My home mail has just come in. I like to be
in the verandah to see the dâk-runner bring in the
letters. I hear him long before I see him, for he
carries a stick with jingling bells at the end to
frighten away animals as he comes through the
jungle. Mine was a particularly nice mail to-day—
good news from everyone. You have no idea how
out here one loves to get letters, and how one

gloats over every scrap of news. Do you really
look forward to my letters? Your letters are the
greatest comfort to me; indeed, I can't imagine
what it would be like without them

I must finish this up, for the mail goes to-morrow.
My time here is nearly run. I hear from Boggley
that he expects to arrive to-morrow, and we depart
together the next day. I shall be sorry and glad
—both. Sorry to leave Takai and the dear people,
more than glad to be with Boggley.

Robert has just come in, excitedly clutching the
tail of a lizard. He had caught it going up the
wall, and the lizard had wriggled away and left
its tail. Now I suppose it will perseveringly grow
another.

Robert is holding the tail before Jean that she
may see it wriggle, and saying, "God made it so.
Wasn't it clever?" The dear babies! How I
shall miss them!

> *Circuit House,*
> *Lakserai, Jan.* 31

THIS letter must begin in pencil, for Boggley has
the only pen. By the bye, would you mind keeping

my letters till I get home ? I think it might be
amusing to read them when my cold weather in
India is a thing of the past.

Behold us on the first stage of our wanderings !

We left Takai on Wednesday, I in my old friend
the doolie, Boggley on his bicycle. It is wonderful
where a bicycle can go in India

I was much sorrier to leave Takai than I thought
I should be, and I think they were a little sorry to
see me go. Even the missionary ladies unbent so
far as to say they would miss my bright face and
merry chatter. How differently people describe
things ! Bright and merry are hardly the adjectives I should have applied to my soulful countenance and brilliant conversation ; but no matter
They all stood on the verandah to watch us go.
Mrs. Russel, dear woman, was obviously sincerely
sorry for anyone leaving such a delectable spot
as Takai ; and indeed there are many worse places
The boys grinned benignly, each hopping on one
foot. Robert, looking rather like a toadstool with
his topi and thin legs, said, " I'm going to Scotland
soon, and I'm not coming back to India till I have
a long beard."

Just as we were starting, an object hurtled through
the air and fell at my feet, and Jean's voice explained,

" It is Topsy, Olivia ; you may have her " ; then, self-sacrificing but heart-broken, she buried her head in her mother's lap   I am rather " tear-minded," as our old nurse used to say, at any time, and I saw things through a mist for the first mile or two.

It didn't seem nearly such a long way going to the station as coming from it, but Boggley on his bicycle was there long before me and my doolie men. We got a train to wherever we were going to about five o'clock. I had some sandwiches with me, and we got tea handed in at a station. It tasted of musty straw, and Boggley said the milk wasn't safe, but the cups made up for everything. Boggley's bore the legend *Forget-me-not*, and mine *A present for a good girl* in gilt letters. About eight o'clock we came to another station—it is quite impossible to remember their ridiculous names—and got out. It was quite an important station, and the large refreshment-room had a long table set for dinner. Lining the walls of the room were tall glass cases filled with tinned meats, jam, biscuits, and other eatables, for in the Mofussil provisions are bought at the railway stations. After dinner Boggley produced a pencil and sheet of paper. " Now," he said, " we must make a list of provisions wanted." So we sat on the table and laid our heads together.

" We'll begin with necessaries," said Boggley
" Butter."

" Jam," I added, " and cheese."

These being put down, we couldn't think of
another single thing.

" Go on," said Boggley, biting his pencil. " That
can't be all."

" Biscuits," I said with a flash of inspiration,
and we chose three boxes of biscuits, and stuck
again

When the attendant produced a list of provisions
kept, we got on better, and soon had two large
wooden boxes packed with things that sounded as
if they might taste good. The only thing I do feel
we have been extravagant in is mustard—it is an
enormous tin, and one doesn't really eat such a vast
deal of mustard.

The list finished and approved, I asked when
our train came in.

" About 4.30," said Boggley.   This was 9 p.m.

" What ! " I cried, aghast. " Where are we
going to sleep ? "

Boggley waved his hands comprehensively.
" Anywhere," he said ; " we'll see what the waiting-
room is like."

The waiting-room was like nothing I had ever

seen before. A large, dirty, barn-like apartment, with some cane seats arranged round the wall, and an attempt at a dressing-table, with a spotty looking-glass on it, in one corner. One small lamp, smelling vilely, served to make darkness visible, and an old hag crouching at the door was the attendant spirit. It doesn't sound cheery, does it? The bearer, Autolycus by name (I call him Autolycus not because he is a knave and witty, but because he is such a snapper-up of unconsidered trifles), made up a bed on one of the cane seats, and there, in that dreary and far from clean apartment, with horrible insects walking up the walls and doubtless carpeting the floor, with no lock on the door and unknown horrors without, I slept dreamlessly. My last waking thought was, " I wish my mother could see me now ! "

Boggley slept in the refreshment-room. Autolycus had gone to the stationmaster and demanded a bed for " a first-class Commissioner Sahib," and, so far does impudence carry one, got it.

I was awakened at 3 a.m., and the aged crone helped me to pack up my bedding. I gave her a rupee, which afterwards I regretted when Autolycus pointed out she had stolen a sheet.

We crossed the Ganges in the grey dawn, a clammy

fog shrouding everything. Nothing was visible but a stretch of wan water, and one or two natives near the bank bathing in the holy river. We were the only Europeans travelling, till at one station a nice old priest came in, of what nationality we couldn't make out. I was pondering it when I discovered that my bangle with the miniature, which I always wear, wasn't on my wrist. We looked up, and down, and round about, and then I shouted, " Why, there it is ! " And there it was lying on the priest's lap. He looked so utterly dumbfoundered, poor dear man, and blushed all over his fat, good-natured face, and I, when I realized I had pointed an accusing finger, was also covered with confusion. We tried to explain that it had come off with my glove, but he merely bowed repeatedly and made hurt ejaculations in some unknown tongue, so we were reduced to an uneasy silence.

About twelve o'clock we had breakfast in the refreshment-room of a station. We had wired for it, so it was ready. First we got ham and eggs. The ham was evidently tinned, and the eggs were quite black. I poked my share suspiciously and asked what made it so black. " Pepper," said Boggley, who was eating away quite placidly.

Pepper ! As if I couldn't recognize plain dirt
when I saw it. Our plates were the kind with
hot water inside, and a cork, and as the venerable
man removed them for the next course I, watching,
saw him wipe them perfunctorily with the corner
of his already none too clean garment, then gravely
hand them back. After that, I thought dry bread
was the safest thing to breakfast on.

Now we are installed in Lakserai Circuit House
These rest-houses are kept up by the Government
for officials on inspection duty. Dâk-bungalows
are rather different. Any traveller may stay . in
them by paying so much. This house consists of
one very large room, dining, drawing, smoking
room in one, and two bedrooms. It is rather damp
and dreary, but that doesn't matter, for we leave
again to-morrow morning. We have been to call
this afternoon on the wife of the Collector, Mrs.
Edston, a pretty woman with nice manners and a
sweet voice. We had tea with her and saw her
small son. Her bungalow interested me. It was
only the second Mofussil bungalow I had seen.
The Takai drawing-room was delightful, a big,
rather empty room, with one or two good repro-
ductions of famous pictures on the walls, heaps of
books, and an almost entire absence of ornaments

—rather an ascetic room. It suited the simple, strenuous life there. Mrs. Edston's is quite different —bright and pretty, full of flowers and growing plants ; tables laden with silver, and photographs of pretty women and children ; comfortable chairs, with opulent cushions, soft rugs and hangings— altogether a very cosy room.

Mrs. Edston has kindly asked us to dine with her to-night.

Later.

We have just come back, and as I am not very sleepy I shall write a bit. It was pouring rain at eight o'clock, so a trap was sent for us, and a note asking us not to whip the horses too hard. I thought they must be very restive animals, but it turned out to be a joke. There were no horses in the trap, only coolies !

We had a very pleasant dinner. Mr. Edston is out in camp, but two young assistant officers were there. They live in tents in the compound, as the bungalow is small, and have their meals with the Edstons. Sitting to-night before a blazing fire, in the pretty drawing-room, listening to Mrs. Edston singing, I reflected that they were exceedingly fortunate young men to have such a home-like habitation and such a charming hostess. To do them justice, I think they quite realize their good fortune.

We depart to-morrow morning for some quite unpronounceable place about twenty miles from here, to stay at another rest-house till Monday.

Madhabad, Sunday.

WE have reached the unpronounceable place after much prayer and fasting. What a day we had yesterday! We left the Lakserai Circuit House at 10 a.m., preceded by Autolycus and a crowd of coolies bearing luggage. Each coolie carries one thing, and as they are all paid the same without regard to the weight carried, of course there is great competition for the light packages. It is odd to see one man stagger under a trunk while another trots gaily off with a cushion or a kodak We are allowed to take hand-luggage into the carriage, and we take such a broad view of the word that it means with us dressing-bags, suit-cases, tennis-rackets, gun-cases, polo-sticks, golf-clubs, and as much more as the compartment will hold.

The station, when we reached it yesterday, was crammed with natives squatting so thick on the

platform one could hardly move without treading
on them. A great festival is going on which only
happens once in a long time—fifty years I think—
and if they bathe in the holy Ganges while
the festival lasts all their sins are washed away.
They are flocking from all parts, eagerly boarding
every train that stops, regardless of the direction
it is going in. The festival ends to-day at twelve,
so I greatly fear many will be disappointed. At
all times the native loves railway travelling, and,
as he has no notion of time-tables, he often arrives
at the station the night before, sleeps peacefully on
the ground, and is in comfortable time for the first
train in the morning. Also, he has no idea of
fixed charges, and when he goes to the ticket-
office and asks for his " tickut," and the babu in
charge tells him the price, he offers half. When
that is refused he goes away, and returns in an
hour or so and offers a little more. It may take
a whole day to convince a native that he can't
beat down the Railway Company.

This festival had so disarranged the trains that
our train which should have left at ten didn't
come in till twelve. Then we had to change at
the next station and wait for the connection, and
we actually sat there till eight in the evening,

when our train sauntered in. They say of a certain
cold and draughty station in Scotland that in it
there is neither man's meat, nor dog's meat, nor a
place to sit down, and it is equally true of the
Indian junction. We had nothing to eat all day
except ginger snaps, and they pall after a time,
especially in a dry and dusty land where no water
is. There were two other travellers in the same
plight, a Mr. and Mrs. Blackie, and we sat together
through that long hot day, too utterly hungry and
bored even to pretend interest in each other.
When the train did come in, something had gone
wrong with the engine, and they lost more time
pottering about with it—tying it up with string
probably. It was then that my temper, and I do
think I behaved with great fortitude up to that
time, gave way, and I tried to bully the officials.
It was no use   They merely smiled and said,
" Cer-tain-lee," and Boggley irritated me more
and more by solemnly repeating ·

> " It is not good for the Christian soul to hustle the
>   Aryan brown,
> For the Christian riles and the heathen smiles
> And it weareth the Christian down
> And the end of the fight is a tombstone white
> With the name of the dear deceased ;
> And the epitaph drear—' A fool lies here
> Who tried to hustle the East.' "

We had nothing to look forward to at the end of the journey except a dâk-bungalow's cold welcome, but the Blackies, who live at Madhabad, insisted we should go home with them to dinner ; so, instead of the tinned ham-and-egg meal we had expected, we had a dainty, well-cooked dinner in a cosy dining-room. Warmed and fed, we retired to our present resting-place, and found little comfort here. Autolycus and his coolies had only just arrived, and Autolycus was searching vainly for a lamp—a *bati* he called it. The floors are stone and as cold as the tomb. Mr. Blackie begged us to go back to his place for the night, but we wouldn't hear of it. Autolycus ran a lamp to earth ; we explored for bedrooms and found two, in which he hastily made up beds. They are damp, and far from clean ; but one learns to put up with a lot in the Mofussil, and in a very short time we had forgotten our troubles in sleep.

This morning I rose betimes and went out to the verandah, and there I found—quite suddenly—a handsome young man. It seems he too is staying in this eligible mansion. He is an engineer—a bridge-builder, I think—and this is convenient for his present work. He was in bed and asleep, and didn't hear us arrive last night ; so he was as

surprised to see me as I was to see him. When
Boggley appeared we had breakfast together. It
was interesting hearing about the kind of life this
young man leads. He says although Madhabad is
not gay, it is Piccadilly compared to where he often
is, out in camp, forty miles from another European,
with not a soul to speak to from week to week. The
evenings are the dreariest times, and he often goes
to bed immediately after dinner. He was quite
cheerful, and said he liked the life. Madhabad
is a large village, but the Blackies are the only
Europeans. There are a lot of planters, however,
living round about. We had callers this morning.
Mr. Royle, to whose place we go on Monday, rode
over with his two small daughters, to say they would
expect us to stay with them. We meant to camp,
but it will be much pleasanter to stay with the
Royles ; everyone says they are charming people.

Boggley and I went for a walk after tea to see the
country. There isn't much to see except a long,
straight brown road and a most insanitary-looking
tank. The village is more interesting with its queer
booths. I do think it is an incongruous sight to
see, as I saw this afternoon, a native, naked but for
a loin cloth, plying a Singer's sewing-machine.
The natives looked sullen and rather suspicious, or is

it only that I imagine it because they are so unlike
the broad-smiling Santals with their cheerful *johar* ?
There are four trees before this bungalow, and at
present two vultures are perching on each—horrible
creatures, with long, scraggy necks.   I pointed them
out to Boggley, who was immediately reminded of
a tale of a bumptious young civilian, new to the
country, who was told, by one who had suffered
many things at his hands, that the birds were wild
turkeys, a much-valued delicacy ; hearing which the
youth promptly shot some and sent them round
to the ladies of the station.   Do you believe that
tale ?   I don't

   . . . We have just finished dinner—much the
most amusing dinner I ever ate.   There is an
intense rivalry, it seems, between our cook and the
engineer-man's cook ; and although we dined together, our bills-of-fare were kept jealously apart.
Autolycus, of course, waited on us, and when he
handed me the fish, and I helped myself to one of
the four pieces, he said sternly, " Two, please,"
and I meekly took the other.   The engineer had
no fish, but on the other hand he had an entrée
which was denied us.   Both cooks rose to a savoury.
(They *will* give you the savoury before the sweet.
If you insist on anything else, it so demoralizes them

that the dinner is a ruin.) Our savoury was rather
ambitious—stuffed eggs rolled in vermicelli. It
tasted rather like a bird's-nest, and one felt it had
taken a lot of making and rolling in brown hands.
I envied the simpler poached egg on tomato of the
engineer. You can't *pat* a poached egg !

Rika, Feb. 9.

I HAVE no home letters to answer this week.
We forgot to give the Calcutta people the new
address, so on Monday night the dâk-runner with
his bells would jingle with my precious home mail
into the Takai verandah ; Mrs. Russel, having
no other address, would re-direct them back to
Calcutta, and they may reach us here about Sunday.
It is tantalizing, but I don't pine for news in Rika
so much as in most places. I am so thoroughly at
home. I find the Mofussil is simply full of nice
people. When we rode out here on Monday morning, and Mrs. Royle, with a shy small girl on either
side, came down the verandah steps to meet us, I
knew I was going to love staying here. There
is an atmosphere about that makes for peace and

11

happiness, and every day I like the place and the people more.

Rika was rather a revelation. The civilians' bungalows have a here-we-have-no-continuing-city look about them ; their owners are constantly being moved, and pitching their moving tents elsewhere ; but the Royles have been at Rika for fifteen years, and have made a delightful home. The bungalow is built on a slightly rising ground with a verandah all round—a verandah made pleasant with comfortable chairs, rugs, writing-tables, books, and flowers. At one end a *dirzee* squats with a sewing-machine, surrounded by white stuff in various stages of progress for the Mem Sahib and the children From the middle of the verandah a broad flight of steps, flanked on either side by growing plants in pots, leads down to the road, and across the road lie the tennis-lawns and the flower-garden. I have read that one of the most pathetic things about this Land of Exile is the useless effort to make English flowers grow. In Rika they must feel at home, for the whole air is scented with roses and mignonette. When Mrs. Royle took us to see her flowers, Boggley pulled a sprig of mignonette, sniffed it appreciatively, and handing it to me said :

  " What does that remind you of ? "

" Miss Aitken's teas ! " I said promptly.

Always that scent takes me straight back to sunny summer afternoons when

> " The day was just a day to my mind,
> All sunny before and sunny behind,
> Over the heather,"

and myself in a stiffly starched frock, accompanied by three brothers with polished faces and spotless collars setting out to drink tea with our friends Miss Aitken and Miss Elspeth.   There was always honey for tea, I remember,—honey made by the bees that buzzed through laborious days in their thatched houses in a corner of the sunny garden,—and little round scones, and crisp shortbread ; and, as we ate and chattered, through the open windows the roses nodded in, giving greeting to their friends, the roses of past summers dried and entombed in great vases ; and the scent of mignonette so mixed itself with the sound of gentle old voices and childish trebles, the fragrant tea in the fragile china cups, the prancing dragons in the cabinet, that now, over the years, it brings them all back to me as surely, as potently, as if it had been indeed a sprig of Oberon's wild thyme or Ophelia's rosemary for remembrance.   As I have told you, we were naughty children, sometimes even wicked children, but our conduct at this house was, "humanly speaking, perfect." The old ladies listened so sympathetically to our tales of how many trout we had that day *guddled* in the burn ; of the colt we had managed to catch and mount—as a family—by the aid of the dyke, and of the few delirious moments spent on its slippery back before it threw us—as a family ; of the ins and outs of why Boggley's nose was swelling visibly and his right eye disappearing. They would look at each other, nodding wisely at intervals while they murmured, "Interestin' bit bairnies." Boggley, when young, was of a peculiarly fiery temper. At times one could hardly look at him without being confronted with squared fists and being invited to "come on " ; but when Miss Elspeth, holding one of his pugnacious paws in her kind, soft hands, assured him he was the flower of the flock, and *her* boy, he was a Samson shorn for mildness.

Speaking pure Lowland Scots, which was a delight to listen to ; full of a gracious hospitality embracing everyone in the district from the highest to the lowest , fiery politicians and ardent supporters of their beloved Free Kirk, to the upkeep of which I believe they would cheerfully have given their last copper, Miss Aitken and Miss Elspeth were of a type now unhappily almost extinct.

Miss Elspeth was the plain, clever one. "In my youth," she loved to quote, "in my youth I wasna what you would ca' bonnie, but I was pale, penetratin', and interestin'."

Miss Aitken had been a beauty, and liked to tell us of the balls she had danced at, when, dressed in white muslin with heelless slippers and a wreath in her hair, she had been called "a sylph." Why she had never married was a puzzle to many. I remember she used to tell us of a wonderful visit to London, and of how she came home sick at heart about leaving all the "ferlies," as she called them. On her first evening at home Miss Elspeth had said, to cheer her, "Come and see the wee pigs." "Me!" said poor Miss Aitken. "What did I care about the wee pigs!" It was, perhaps, more than the "ferlies" she missed, but I don't know. She was no sylph when I knew her, my dear Miss Aitken, but she had a most comfortable lap, and a cap with cherry ribbons, and the kindest heart in all the world. Once, John, who thirsted always for information, and mindful of a point that had struck him in the chapter at morning prayers, said:

"Miss Aitken, are you any relation to Achan-in-the-Camp?"

Miss Elspeth, looking quizzically at her sister,

answered for her: " Dod! Marget, I wouldna
wonder but what ye micht hae been tempted by the
Babylonish garment!"

They were very old when we knew them, these
dear ladies, and they have been dead many years,
but their simple, kindly lives have left a fragrance
to sweeten this workaday world even as the mignonette in bygone summers scented their old-world
garden.

How I do reminisce! It is entirely your fault for
saying you liked it. You know it is a trait in the
Douglas family. Our way of entertaining guests
is to sit close together and recall happenings,
and delightedly remind each other of childish es-
capades, shouting hilariously, while our guests sit in
a bored and puzzled silence. Pleasant family the
Douglases!

Well, as I said, Rika is a pleasant place and the
Royles Irish, therefore charming. Mrs. Royle is a
most purpose-like person. I like to go with her in
the morning on her rounds. Through the gardens
we go to see the bananas and pine-apples and
tomatoes ripening in the sun, and make sure that
the *malis* are doing their work ; then on to the wash-
house, where the *dhobi* is finishing the weekly wash ;
to the kitchens, to see that the cooking-pots are

clean ; finally, to stand on the verandah while the *syces* bring the ponies and feed them before our suspicious eyes. I forgot the henhouse. As we live almost entirely on fowls in the Mofussil, the *moorghy-khana* is a most important feature of the establishment ; but just now, I regret to say, owing to a moorghy famine in the district, the stock is at a somewhat low ebb. Men have been scouring the country for fowls, but when we went to look at the result this morning we found about a dozen miserable chickens, almost featherless, standing dejectedly in corners, and Mrs. Royle wailed, " We can't kill these : it would be a sheer slaughter of the innocents ! " It isn't easy to get beef or mutton in this part of the world, and when a sheep is brought to Rika it has to be carefully concealed, or Kittiwake ties a ribbon round its neck and claims it as her own, and terrible is the outcry if anyone dares to make away with her pet.

There are two Royle children—Kittiwake and Hilda. Kittiwake (christened, I believe, Kathleen Helen) is fat and broad and beaming, and very religious. Hilda is inclined to love the gay world, and finds Rika too quiet—the baby aged six ! They are both thorough little sportsmen and mounted on their ponies go with their father almost everywhere.

Yesterday I went for a ride with them, along dusty brown roads between rice-fields, and they gave me a wonderful lot of information about the place and the people. As we passed a little village temple Kittiwake stopped. " *That,*" she said solemnly, pointing with her whip, " is where they worship false gods."

I told Mr. Royle about Peter being so anxious for a mongoose, and to-day when the children came running to beg me to come quickly and see what the fisherman had caught for me, my mind leapt at once to mongooses. When I saw, confined under a wicker basket, two animals with yellow fur and flat heads that moved ceaselessly, my heart sank. If they had been caught for me how could I be so ungracious as to refuse them, and yet how was it possible for me to carry these most terrifying creatures about with me, and perhaps, on the voyage home, have to share my cabin with them ?

I looked round wildly. The fisherman was grinning delightedly at his own cleverness. Our two *chuprassis,* Autolycus, and a *syce* stood round with the children, all waiting for my approval.

" They're rather nice, aren't they ? " I stammered feebly.

" Oh—*sweet !* " said Hilda rapturously.

"Sweet!" I echoed. "But aren't they big ones?"

"Big!" cried Kittiwake "Why, they're only *butchas*;" and she lifted the edge of the basket to get a better view, at which one of the *butchas* made a rush for the opening and made straight at me. With a yell I snatched up my skirts, knocked over Hilda, leapt "like a haarse" on to the verandah straight into the astonished Mr. Royle, while the weird beast disappeared like a yellow streak.

"Whatever is the matter?" he asked as I sank to the floor.

"Olivia's afraid of the *butcha* otter!" squealed Hilda, while she scampered about looking for the truant.

"Otter?" said I.

"Yes," said Mr. Royle; "they are baby otters that the fisherman found at the side of the lake. I thought of sending them to the Calcutta Zoo. They aren't very common in India."

"I'm *so* glad!" I gasped; and Mr. Royle looked mystified. It didn't seem exactly a reason for fervent gladness, but suppose they *had* been mongooses? My life, so to speak, was ruined.

Staying in the house with Mr. Royle is rather like being with Colonel Newcome in the flesh. He

is such a very "perfect gentil Knight"—as courteous
to a native woman as to the L.-G.'s wife.   The
people round about adore him and his wife ; they
are a kind of father and mother to the whole district.   There would be little heard of disloyalty to
the British if all the Sahibs were like Mr. Royle.
He is so good—I'd be almost afraid to be so good
in case I died—but not the least in a sickly way.
He is a teetotaller, a thing almost unheard of in
India ; and he isn't ashamed to be heard singing
hymns with the children before their bed-time ;
yet (why yet ?) he is a crack shot, a fine polo
player, an all-round sportsman.

Both he and his wife are very fond of books
Mrs. Royle reads everything she can lay her hands
on, but her husband's special subject is philosophy,
and last night he lent me a volume of Nietzsche.
I don't think I understood a single word, but
between it and the *moorghy-khana* I had a bad
night.   I thought I had to make in five minutes
a new scheme of the Universe.   All the odd-shaped
pieces were lying about like a picture-puzzle, and
I feverishly tried to make them fit, in the clumsy
ineffective way one does things in dreams.   Just
as I had it almost finished, Mrs. Royle came with a
fowl in each hand and said sternly, " These must

come into your scheme." I took the two great
clucking things and vainly tried to thrust their feet
—or is it claws hens have?—into a tiny corner,
and they had just wrecked all my efforts when I
woke !

I have taken some photographs which I shall send
you. The delightful babu buttoned tightly into
the frock-coat is a clerk of Mr. Royle's, called a
" Sita-Ram—two-o'clock." The frock-coat was a
legacy from a departing Collector, and he is immensely proud of it.   He is a great delight to me,
and says he will never cease to pray for my *internal*
welfare! Talking of babus, one wrote to Mr.
Royle the other day about a pair of riding-breeches,
and said, " I have your Honour's measurements,
but will be glad to know if there is any improve-
ment in the girth." Don't you think that was a
very pretty way of asking if he had put on weight ?
    When I showed Autolycus and the *chuprassis*
the photographs I had taken of them, the *chuprassis*
said, " *Atcha* " (very good), but Autolycus shook
his head violently, and when Boggley asked him
what was wrong, he replied in an injured tone
that it made him look quite black !

. . DEEP snow, hard frost, bright sun—how gloriously sparkling it must be! It dazzles my eyes to think of it   I don't wonder you revel in the skating and the long sleigh rides through the silent forest. Talk about the magic of the East—it could never appeal to me like the magic of the North.

Storks, snow-queens, moor-wives, ell-women— how the names thrill one! What was your Hans Andersen like? Mine was light blue and gold with wonderful coloured pictures, but it was the frontispiece I studied, and which held me frightened yet fascinated. It was a picture of a pine-wood, with a small girl in a blue frock and white pinafore and red stockings, crying bitterly under a tree, in the branch of which a doll hung limply, thrown there by cruel brothers. Through the trees the sunset sky was pale green melting into rose-colour, and the wicked little gnomes that twilight brings were tweaking the child's hair and jeering at her misfortunes. One felt how cold it was, and how badly the little girl wanted her hood and cloak. The darkness was very near, and worse things than little gnomes would slip from behind the tree-

trunks. It never occurred to me that the little
girl might have run home to warmth and light and
safety. That was no solution—the doll would still
have been there. Your letter, with its tale of snow
and great quiet forests, and the picture you drew
me of the funny little girl with the flaxen plaits
and the red stockings, made me remember it. I
don't know where my old book is—gone long since
from the nursery bookshelf to the dustbin, I expect,
for it was much-used and frail when I 'knew and
loved it—but your word-picture gave me the pass-
port and enabled me to creep once again inside its
cover, so brave in blue and gold, and to greet my
friend in the red stockings, and find her as highly
coloured as ever, and not a day older. It is nice
of you to say I have a courageous outlook on life,
but I wish I hadn't told you the story of the mongoose that was an otter. Now you will say, like
Boggley, *Funk-stick!* If I stay much longer in
this frightsome land my hair will be white and my
nervous system a mere wreck.

Yesterday we left the solitude of Rika and went
to polo at a place about seventeen miles away.
It was very interesting to meet all the neighbour-
ing Europeans—mostly planters and their wives.
There were about twenty people, and everyone

very nice. I wish I had time to tell you about
them, but I haven't. After polo, which I enjoyed
watching, we all had tea together and talked very
affably. Then Mr. Royle drove me home while
Boggley went with Mrs. Royle. I heard, as we
were leaving, Mr. Royle say something to Boggley
about the horse being young and skittish, and a
faint misgiving passed through me, but I forgot it
talking to Mr. Royle, and when we reached Rika
I went off to dress for dinner, taking it for granted
that the others were just behind. Letters were
waiting me, and I lingered so long over them I had
to dress in a hurry, and ran to the drawing-room
expecting to find everyone waiting. But the
room was empty. Hungry and puzzled, I waited
for another ten minutes, and then went along to
Boggley's bedroom, to see what *he* meant anyway
but there was no one there. More and more
puzzled, but distinctly less hungry, I went back
to the drawing-room, looked into the dining room,
finally wandered out into the verandah, where I
found the children's old nurse Anne tidying away
the children's toys.

I said : " Nurse, where's everybody ? "

Anne left the toys and lifted both hands to high
heaven.

"Och ! Miss Douglas dear, it wasn't for nothing
I dreamt last night of water-horses. The night
before ma sister Maggie's man was killed by a kick
from a wicked grey horse (Angus M'Vcecar was
his name, and a fine young lad he was) I dreamt I
saw one.   As big as three hills it was, with an awful
starin' white face, and a tail on it near as long as
from Portree to Sligachen.   It give a great screech,
and a wallop in the face of me, and jumped into
the loch, and by milkin'-time next morning—a
Thursday it was—ma sister Maggie came into the
door cryin', ' Och and och, ma poor man, and him
so kind and so young,' and fell on the floor as stiff
as a board."

Anne comes from Skye, and often tells me about
water-horses and such-like odd denizens of that
far island ; and I find her soft Highland speech,
with its " ass " for " as " and " ch " for " j," very
diverting ; but this time I wasn't amused.

"But nothing *has* happened, Anne. What are
you talking about ?   Where is my brother ? "

" Mercy on us all, how can I tell ?   The mistress
and the young gentleman has never come in, and
the master says to me, ' Fetch me my flask, Anne,'
says he ; and fetch it I did, and he drove away, an'
I'm sure as I'm sittin' here I didn't see the water-

horse for nothing   What does a flask mean but
an accident ? Och—och, and a nice laughin'-faced
young gentleman he was, too."

If life is going to contain many such half-hours
I don't see how I am to get through it with any
credit.   I left Anne—whom at that moment I
hated—to seek information from the servants, which
she did with a valiant disregard of her entire lack
of knowledge of Hindustani, a language she stub-
bornly refused to learn a word of.   The last I saw
of her she had seized the *khansamah's* young assistant and was shouting at him, "Chokra—ye impident
little black deevil, will you tell this moment, has
there been an accident ? "   Backwards and forwards I went in the verandah, then down the steps
to the road, straining my eyes to see and my ears
to hear something—what I did not know.   From the
garden the scent of the roses and mignonette came
to me in the soft Indian darkness.   I ventured a
little bit along the road, too anxious to remember,
or, remembering, to care, that I had no lantern,
and that at any moment I might tread on a snake.
I could only think of one thing, and how often I
pictured it ! Mr. Royle coming back, and the
natives carrying someone—someone who didn't
laugh any more.   The odd thing was I didn't

seem to mind at all what happened to kind Mrs.
Royle. It was Boggley, and only Boggley, that
mattered to me. Of course nothing did happen
to anyone   It isn't when one expects and dreads
it that tragedy comes. Tragedy comes quietly,
swiftly. I remember going to see a fisherman's
widow in a little village on the stormy east coast.
She told me of her husband's death. " I had his
tea a' ready an' a bit buttered toast an' a kipper,
but he never cam' in."   That was all—" He never
cam' in."

When our wanderers returned they were rather
amused than otherwise. The horse had given
trouble and ended by kicking the trap to pieces,
and they had to walk part of the way home. Quite
simple, you see ; but the first opportunity I looked
in a mirror to see if my hair had not turned white
in a single night, as men's have done through sudden
fear. It hadn't ; but I did dream of a water-
horse with " an awful starin' white face."

This morning Mrs. Royle took me to the village
to get some brass to take home. The shop was a
little hut with an earthen floor, a pair of scales, and
one shelf crowded with brass things, made, not for
the European market, but for the daily use of the
people, such as drinking-vessels—*lota* is the pretty

12

name—and big brass plates out of which they eat their rice and *dhalbat*. They keep them beautifully polished with sand, and I think they ought to be rather decorative ; much more attractive certainly than the candlesticks and pots and cheap rough silver-work which is the usual loot carried away by the cold-weather visitor.

16th.

ANOTHER mail-day will soon be upon us ; they simply pounce on one. We have to get letters away by Tuesday from the Mofussil instead of Thursday as in Calcutta. I look forward with great distaste to leaving this place next week. When with the Royles one can't imagine oneself happy anywhere else. The days pass so quickly ; breakfast seems hardly over when it is time for luncheon, and before one has really settled down to read or write it is four o'clock, and time to go to tea, which is spread down by the lake among the roses, the sun having lost its fierceness and begun to think of going to bed. We all sit at a round table and eat brown bread and butter and jam, all home-made. The china we use is very pretty and came from Ireland, but Mrs. Royle has been greatly troubled by its

discoloured appearance, which the servants assured
her there was no cure for. I suggested rough salt
and lemon-juice, and after tea yesterday afternoon
they brought it, and we each set to work on our own
cup and saucer, and behold ! in a very short time
they were like new. Boggley made his particularly
beautiful, but unfortunately broke it immediately
afterwards, at which Kittiwake laughed so im-
moderately she fell on her saucer and sent it to its
long home.

I have learned to take a most intelligent interest
in fowls and Nietzsche ; and more and more as the
days pass do I like and admire our host and hostess.
I never met people I felt so *affectionately* towards.

Here come the children flying, followed patiently
by the old *khansamah* with a spoon in one hand and
a bottle of cod-liver-oil emulsion in the other. I
had better finish this letter and get the ink out
of their reach.

Baratah, Thursday, Feb. 21.

. . Now we are really camping out, and I sit
outside my tent even as Abraham did of old. I
have a whole long day before me to write. Boggley

was up and away long before I was awake, and won't
be back till evening.

We left Rika on Monday afternoon, very sad
indeed. Mrs Royle, as is her way, heaped us with
benefits, and, mindful of our starvation on the way
to Rika, had a luncheon-basket packed with cold
fowl, home-made bread, tomatoes, and a big cake.
As we drove off the children pursued us down the
drive crying, "Don't go away. Stay with us
always." '

At the station we were told that the train was
two hours late, and Boggley thought it would be an
excellent plan to spend the time calling on the
Blackies, who live near ; so, leaving Autolycus and
the *chuprassis* with the luggage, we set out. We
had been shown the flower-garden and a crocodile
that Mr. Blackie had shot, and were about to drink
a dish of tea in the drawing-room, when we heard
the whistle of an engine. "The train !" cried
Boggley, bounding to his feet, and spurning the
cup of tea Mrs. Blackie was offering to him. It
was no moment for ceremony. With a shrieked
good-bye we leapt out of the window and across the
compound, and set off on our half-mile run to the
station. There is something peculiarly nasty about
the nature of Indian trains. Simply because we

left the station it chose to be up to time. It must
have been an amusing incident to the people in the
station, but I would have enjoyed it more had I been
one of the natives watching from a third-class
carriage instead of, so to speak, one of the principal
actors. There was the engine shrieking in its
anxiety to start; there was our luggage neatly
spread all over an empty compartment; there was
Autolycus protesting shrilly that the train could
not leave without his sahib, who was a very *burra*
sahib; and finally there *we* were with scarlet faces,
topis on the backs of our heads, surrounded by a
thick cloud of dust, careering wildly into the station.

After all the fuss, we had only about thirty miles
to travel, when we got out and drove three miles
in a kind of native cart to a dâk-bungalow, a very
poor and uncomfortable specimen of its kind. It
didn't uplift us to hear that plague was very bad
all round, and after a somewhat jungly dinner
during which we were very thoughtful and disin-
clined for conversation, we sought our mildewed
couches, to rise again at skreich of day and continue
our journey, till late on Tuesday night we got out
finally at Baratah station and drove out to our
present camping-ground. The people knew we were
coming, and the tents were up; but they hadn't

expected us till the next day, so nothing was ready,
not even a lamp. It was the oddest experience to
stumble about in black darkness in entirely unknown surroundings   You know how Boggley
tumbles over things in the broad light of day, so
you can imagine what tosses he took over dressing-
tables and chairs in the darkness.   It didn't last
long, however, for an important fat *khansamah*
hurried in, shocked at our plight, and, explaining
that his sahib, Mr. Lister, was away for a few days,
brought us a lamp and other necessaries.   Dinner
was not possible under the circumstances—the
box with our forks and knives had not arrived—
so the remains of Mrs. Royle's luncheon-basket
coldly furnished forth our evening meal.   While
we sat there, uncomfortably poised on dressing-
bags, gnawing legs of fowl and hunches of bread, I
thought of you probably dining at the Ritz or the
Savoy, with soft lights and music, and lovely food,
and probably not half as merry as Boggley and I.

I don't know if I really like a tent to live in.
The floor is covered with straw, and then a carpet
is stretched over it, which makes a particularly
bulgy, uneven surface to stand dressing-tables and
things on.   The straw, too, is apt to stick out
where it is least expected, and gives one rather

the feeling of being a tinker sleeping in a barn. At
night a tent is an awesome place. It is terrible
to have no door to lock, and to be entirely at the
mercy of anything that creeps and crawls , to have
only a mosquito-net between you and an awful
end. I woke last night to hear something sniffing
outside the tent. It scraped and scraped, and I
was sure that it was digging a hole and creeping
underneath the canvas. I sat up in bed and in a
quavering voice said " Go away," and the noise
stopped, but only to begin again—scrape, scrape,
snuffle, snuffle, in the most eerie way. Then something worse happened. At my very ear, as it
seemed, the most blood-curdling yell rent the
astonished air. It was only a jackal, Boggley
says, but it sounded as if all the forces of evil had
been let loose at once. You can laugh if you like,
but I think it was enough to frighten a very Daniel.
As for me, in one moment I was well under the
blankets, with fingers in both ears, and I suppose
even in the midst of my terror I must have fallen
asleep, for the next thing I knew was daylight
and the cheerful sound of voices. To-night I
shall have a lamp burning and a *chokidar* (watch-
man) to sleep outside my tent.

Baratah is quite a large town, and has a Roman

Catholic Mission and two lady doctors. We are camping about a mile from the town in a corner of Mr. Lister's compound. It is pretty, with well-kept grass and flower-beds, and opposite is the Guest House of the Raj, where we would be staying now were it not that its roof is not quite safe, and it cannot be used. I went through it, and a great neglected place it is, with tawdry Early Victorian furniture and awful oleographs.

When the sun had gone down yesterday, we went for a walk to explore, along an avenue of peepul trees, across a fine polo-ground, and then we lighted on a big tank. A tiny native boy was perched on the bank watching something in the water, so we sat down beside him and watched too. The something was very large and black, and we were puzzled to know what it was, till, at a word from the child, it heaved itself out of the water and revealed itself an elephant. Up it came to where we were, laid its trunk down so that the small boy could walk up, and off he went proudly riding on its head. It was the nicest thing to watch I ever saw.

We got the home mail the night we arrived here, but couldn't see to read it till the next morning. So you are back in London—sloppy, muggy, February

London ! How you will miss the cold clear North and all the ice-fun ; but you will be so busy finishing the book that surroundings won't matter much. It seemed quite home-like to see the familiar address on the note-paper.

To-day I am going to devote entirely to writing. Surely my book will make some progress now. How many words should there be in a book ? I've got 18,000 now ; " ragged incompetent words " they are, too. I wonder what makes a writer of books ! Would knowing all the words in the dictionary help me ? My statements are so bald, somehow It doesn't seem an interesting tale to me, so I'm afraid I can't expect an unprejudiced reader to find it thrilling. The Mutiny is perhaps too large a subject for me—though, mind you, there is one bit that sounds rather well. I have taken great pains with it, and, as Viola said of her declaration, " 'tis poetical ! " The worst of it is, when I write poetically I am never quite sure that I am writing sense. I dare say I would be wise to take the Moorwife's advice. You remember in *The Will-o'-the Wisps are in Town*, when the man had listened to the Moorwife's tale he said, " I might write a book about that, a novel in twelve volumes, or better, a popular play."

" Or better still," said the Moorwife, " you might let it alone."

" Ah," said the man, " that would be pleasanter and easier."

How true !

Baratah, Thursday, Feb. 28.

WE are still in Baratah, as you see, and shall be till Tuesday. It is a very nice life this nomadic existence, and one gets nearer the people. They come in little groups and talk to Boggley outside his tent, and I must say he is most patient with them and tries to do his very best for each one of them. They make my heart ache, these natives, they are so gentle and so desperately poor. Isn't it Steevens who says the Indian ryot has been starving for thirty centuries and sees no reason why he should be filled ?

The Listers are home now and we have been seeing a lot of them. They are delightful people Mrs. Lister is quite a girl, and so good-looking and cheery. She has the prettiest house I think I ever saw. When we went to call the first time and were shown into the white-panelled drawing-

room with its great open blue-tiled fireplace and
cupboards of blue china, I suppose it was the
contrast with our own rather sordid surroundings,
but it seemed to me like fairyland. The hall is
lovely, with a gallery all round and most exquisite
carving; rose-red velvet curtains, Persian rugs
glowing with rich, soft colours, and everywhere
great silver bowls of flowers. They are the most
hospitable people, and ask us to dinner every night,
and to every other meal as well Mr. Lister told
me babu stories last night. Here is one. The
Government sent round making inquiries about
some Scandinavians. (Please don't ask why
Scandinavians, because I can't answer.) The Sub-
Divisional Officer forwarded the reference to the
different police-stations for report. The babus in
charge of these stations hadn't an idea what
Scandinavians were, but would have scorned to ask
Three of the reports ran thus :

>   1. " Honoured Sir, I have the honour to report
>   that the Scandinavian has been concluded
>   in this district and has been removed to
>   Lahserai." (Survey and Settlement opera-
>   tions.)
>   2. " Sir, I have the honour to report that there

has been no Scandinavians in the district
this year, but it is raging furiously at Rıka."
(Plague.)

3. " Sir, I have the honour to report two Scandinavians were seen at Gopalbung. One
was shot by Billie Burke Sahib, the other has
not since returned." (Tigers.)

That is a good, but somewhat involved, story.
Another was about a missionary who had been
eaten by a tiger. The police wired, " A tiger has
man-eaten the Pope of Ramnugger."

Yesterday the Listers had a duck-shoot. About
twenty men came from all round, and Mrs. Lister
and I went with them. We drove two and two to
a very large lake and then set sail in queer native
boats punted by natives. Of course I wanted to
go with Boggley, but was sent off with a strange
man, one Major Griffiths, who eyed me with great
dislike because he said my light dress would frighten
the birds. It got frightfully hot with the sun beating on the water, and I simply dared not put up
a sunshade in case of scaring the birds more than
I was already doing, and thereby increasing the
wrath of my companion. He shot a lot of ducks,
but evidently not so many as he thought he ought

to shoot, and when he saw the birds all congregated at one corner of the lake a thought struck him, and he told the natives to take us to shore. He got out and beckoned me to follow, which I obediently did, and together we crawled through the jungle, with the *bandar-log* chattering above us and—for all I know to the contrary—snakes hissing beneath our feet. If I stepped, which I could hardly avoid doing sometimes, on a fallen branch, making it crackle, the man turned on me a glance so malignant I positively quailed. Breathlessly we crept to the water-side and the unsuspecting ducks, and then Major Griffiths fired into the brown,—is that the proper expression?—killing I don't know how many. I don't think it was at all a nice thing to do, but my opinion was neither asked nor desired. Even then my friend was not satisfied, and he voyaged about until I knew luncheon was long since a thing of the past, and I hated so the shape of his face I could have screamed. When at last we did return, I found my surmise as to luncheon had been only too correct, and we had to content ourselves with scraps. The next duck-shoot I attend I shall choose as companion a less earnest sportsman.

The weather is beginning to stoke-up, as Boggley calls it, and during the day the tent is insufferable.

I can sit outside it in the early morning, but as the sun gets up Autolycus summons the *chuprassis*, and they carry my table and writing-materials to the verandah of the Guest House, which has a cool, not to say clammy and tomb-like, atmosphere. My chief trials are the insects   There is a kind of large black beetle with wings that has a strange habit of poising itself just above my head and remaining there. Someone told me—who I forget ; anyway, Boggley says it isn't true, but it seems quite likely—that if these beetles drop on you they *explode.* Did you ever hear of anything quite so horrible ? I keep a wary eye on them and shift my seat at their approach.

Not a hundred yards away a heathen temple stands, with its gilded roof shining in the sun. We tried to go inside it the other day, but an angel with a flaming sword, in the shape of a *fakir*, kept us out. It didn't look very attractive. We saw enough when we beheld the post the poor kids and goats are tied to, all messy and horrid from the last·sacrifice. The priest who forbade us to enter, just to show there was no ill-feeling, hung wreaths of marigolds round our necks. Boggley, once we were out of sight, hid his in the ditch ; but I, afraid they might find out and be offended, went about for the rest of the day decked like any sacrificial goat.

That we are leading the Simple Life I think you would admit if you saw us at our meals I find that food really matters very little. Our cook is of the jungle jungly. Autolycus is disgusted with him, and does his best to reform him. *Chota-hazri* I have alone, as Boggley is away inspecting before seven o'clock. I emerge from my tent and find a table before Boggley's tent with a cloth on it,—not particularly clean,—a loaf of bread (our bread is made in jail : a *chuprassi* goes to fetch it every second day), a tin of butter, and a tin of jam. Autolycus appears accompanied by the jungly cook, bearing a plate of what under happier cir- cumstances might have been porridge. A spoonful or two is more than enough. " No good ? " demands Autolycus. " No," and disdainfully handing the plate back to the entirely indifferent cook, he pro- ceeds to produce from somewhere about his person a teapot and two tiny eggs. Luncheon is much worse, for the food that appears is so incalcul- ably greasy that it argues a more than bowing acquaintance with native *ghee*. Dinner is luncheon intensified, so tea is really the only thing we can enjoy. The fact is, if we thought about it we would

never eat at all. I happened to walk round the
tent to-day, and found the dish-washer washing
our dishes in water that was positively thick, and
drying them with a cloth that had begun life polish-
ing our brown boots. I stormed at him in English,
and later Boggley stormed at him in Hindustani,
and he vowed it would never happen again ; but I
dare say if I were to look round at this minute, I
should find him doing exactly the same thing ;
and I don't really care so long as neither of us
perishes with cholera as a result.

Such funny things live behind my tent ! What
should I find the other day but a little native baby
—about two or three years old. It seems his mother
is dead, and his father, who is our *chokidar*, has to
take him with him wherever he goes. He is the
oddest little figure, clothed in a most inadequate
shirt, and a string round his neck with a shell
attached to keep away evil spirits. His hair is
closely shaved except for one upstanding tuft
which is left to pull him up to heaven with ; and
his face looks nothing but two great twinkling
eyes. He squats beside me nearly all day, and
eagerly eats anything I give him, like a little puppy
dog. Toffee and fancy biscuits, both of which I
possess in abundance, are his favourites. An old

servant of Boggley's is with a sahib near here, and he arrived dressed in spotless white from head to foot, bearing in one hand a large seed cake wreathed with marigolds, and in the other a plate of toffee coloured pink, green. and yellow, an offering to the Miss Sahib which he presented with many salaams, and of which my little Hindoo gets the benefit. Autolycus and the *chuprassis* take a great interest in teaching him manners. When I hold out a biscuit Autolycus says sternly, " Say salaam to the Miss Sahib," and the baby puts his small hand gravely to his forehead, bowing low with a " Talaam, Mees Tahib," then snaps up the prize. I shall miss my little companion   I wonder what will become of him—little brown heir of the ages. Already he can lisp to idols, but he has never even heard of the Christ who said, " Suffer the children."

March 3.

I SHALL finish this and post it to-morrow before we leave. We have been to church to-night, the most unusual occurrence with us nowadays. Of course it was only an English church (I remember the time when I thought it very exciting and more than a little wicked to be present at a Church of England

13

service) and the padre was a very little young padre,
and rather depressing. He insisted so that we
were but a passing vapour that I began to feel it was
only too horribly true, and Boggley, who had par-
taken largely of tinned cheese at luncheon and was
feeling far from well, grew every moment more
yellow and green.

The Listers asked us to go back with them to
dinner, but we thought it better (Boggley especially) to seek the seclusion of our tents.

Manpur, March 9.

Now we are in a different place. At least it has
a different name and is a day's journey from Ban
tale, but it looks exactly the same. We left Baratah
yesterday morning and got in and out of trains all
day until about seven in the evening we got out finally
at Manpur. I had a dreadful cold, and was sniffy
and inclined to be cross ; so when Boggley suggested
we should dine in the waiting-room while Autolycus and the *chuprassis* went on with the luggage
to acquaint the dâk-bungalow people of our arrival,
I upbraided him for not making proper arrange-

ments, and reviled the meagre repast, and was
altogether very unpleasant.   When we reached
our destination we found Autolycus prancing dis-
tractedly   " This," he said to Boggley, " is what
comes of making no bundabust." · Some other
people were already occupying the bungalow, and
we could only get the back rooms, small, mouldy, and
inconvenient.   Poor Boggley looked so crushed I had
to laugh, and we calmed the worried Autolycus, who
hates to see his Sahib shoved into corners, and, there
being no inducement to remain up—went to bed.

Manpur is a fairly big station—the sort of place
you read about in Anglo-Indian novels   There are
six households and a club.   Boggley and I called
on all the six this evening, and then went to the club.
Everyone meets there in the evening to see the
picture-papers and to play tennis and bridge.

It is rather a bored little community, Manpur.
I think they are all pretty sick of each other, and one
can't wonder.   Even an Archangel would pall if one
met him at tea, played tennis with him, and sat
next him at dinner almost every day of the year ;
how much more poor human beings—and Anglo-
Indian human beings at that.   Taken separately
they are delightful, but each assures us that the
others are quite impossible.   They unite in being

shocked at our living in such discomfort, and have all invited us to stay; but it isn't worth while to change our quarters. Besides, we are going away for the week-end to some friend of Boggley's who lives about thirty miles from here.

A nice little young civilian is at present calling on us. He came to pay his duty call, and he and Boggley became so deep in Oxford talk, and found so many mutual friends, that we asked him to stay to dinner. Autolycus told me in a stage whisper that the Sahib could easily stay as the dâk-bungalow cook was very good, and that we would get quite a Calcutta dinner. His pride, as he bore in the dishes, was beautiful to see; and it was a good dinner, though rather tinny.

Manpur, Thursday 12th

THIS delayed letter must be posted before we leave by the night train for our next trek. We came back late last night from Misanpore after a nice but very queer time. On Saturday, when, after a long dusty drive of eight miles from the station, we arrived at the bungalow of Boggley's friend, there was every evidence that no visitors were expected. Just think! Boggley had never let him know we were

coming; the poor man was ignorant of the fearful
joy in store for him.

I gripped Boggley by the arm. "Wretch," I
hissed in his ear. "Why didn't you write? What
sort of man is he? Will he hate having me?"

"*Qui hai?*" bellowed Boggley to the deserted-
looking bungalow. Then, turning to me, "Oh yes,
he'll hate it," he said calmly; "but he'll be pleased
afterwards." I could have shaken him. Making
me play the part of a visit to the dentist.

When our host appeared, very dishevelled (it
turned out that he was feeling far from well and
had been lying down), and beheld me, dismay was
written large on his countenance He glared
round in a hunted way, and it looked as if he were
going to make a bolt for it, but he remembered in
time his manhood, and faced me. (His name is
Ferris, and he is tall and bald, and about forty,
and so shy that when he blushes his eyes water.)
Somehow, we all got inside the house, and Boggley
and I sat in the drawing-room while Mr. Ferris
rushed out to summon his minions and make arrange-
ments. We heard a whispered discussion going on
about sheets, and I longed to tell my distracted
host that I had all my bedding with me in a strap;
but the thought that he might consider me " on-

delicate," like Mr. Glegg, deterred me. Presently I was shown into what, only too evidently, was our host's own room, for a servant snatched away some last remaining effects of his master—a spatter-brush and a slipper—as I entered. I sat down on the bed and pondered over what I would have felt had I been a man, and shy, and seedy, and a strange female had been suddenly shot into my peaceful home.

It was rather a difficult week-end. I have met men who were difficult to talk to, but never one like Mr. Ferris, who, while willing, indeed anxious, to be agreeable, so absolutely annihilated conversation. It wasn't till dinner on Sunday night that I discovered a subject that really interested him—London restaurants. He grew quite animated as we discussed the relative merits of the Ritz, the Carlton, the Savoy, the Dieudonné. I think that long, thin, bald, gentle bachelor spends all his spare moments—and he must have many in lonely Misanpore—thinking about his next leave and the feasts he will then enjoy. Yet the odd thing is he isn't greedy about food. I think it must be more the lights and music and people that attract him.

Mr. Ferris and Boggley were away all Sunday,

and I spent the whole day with a volume of Dana
Gibson's drawings, the only book I could find. I
did go for a short walk, but the dust was nearly
knee-deep, and, except the little bungalow and
outhouses, there was absolutely nothing to see.

Yesterday again Boggley had to go and inspect
some place, so it was decided he would bicycle
there, and then pick me up at some station we had
to change at on our way to Manpur. I drove to
the station in Mr. Ferris's little dogcart—alone.
Mr. Ferris said he was so sorry he had an engage-
ment, but I think myself it was simply that he
couldn't face the eight miles alone with me.

The groom, instead of sitting behind, ran behind,
and as the pony was fresh he had to run pretty
fast. There were two roads—a *pukka* or made road,
and a *cutcha* road, on which the natives walked and
drove their *ekkas*.

Autolycus and the *chuprassis* were waiting at
the station, and put me into a carriage. They
went straight on to Manpur with the luggage
instead of waiting at the station where we changed
trains. It was ten o'clock when I got out of the
train, and Boggley had said he would be no later
than half-past eleven ; then we would have luncheon,
and get the one o'clock train to Manpur. I went

into the refreshment-room to ask what we could
have for luncheon.

" Ham and eggs," said the fat babu promptly.

" Nothing else ? " I asked

" Yes," said the babu ; " mixed biscuits."

" Oh," I said, surprised.

" Certainlee," said the babu.

Then I went outside to read a book and watch
for Boggley. My book was one of those American
novels where every woman is—to judge from the
illustrations—of more than earthly beauty. I got so
disheartened after a little when everyone I met had
a complexion of rose and snow (besides, I didn't
believe it) that I shut it up. I found it was nearly
twelve o'clock, and Boggley hadn't arrived. I
waited another quarter of an hour, and then went
in and ate some ham and eggs. One o'clock, and
the train came and went, but still no trace of the
laggard. Outside the station the blinding white
road lay empty. Nothing stirred, not even a
native was visible ; the whole world seemed asleep
in the heat   A pile of trunks lay on the platform
addressed to somewhere in Devonshire and labelled
Not wanted on the Voyage. Some happy people
were going home. A far cry it seemed from this
dusty land to green Devonshire. I sat on the

largest trunk and thought about it.   Two o'clock,
three, four—the hours went past.   I felt myself
becoming exactly like a native, sitting with my
hands folded, looking straight before me.   If I
hadn't been so anxious I shouldn't have minded
the waiting at all.   Now and again I refreshed myself
with a peep at the babu, just to assure myself that
I wasn't the only person left alive in the world.

About five o'clock Boggley and his bicycle strolled
into the station.   I had meant to be frightfully
cross with him when he appeared—that is to say,
if he weren't wounded or disabled in any way—but
somehow I never can be very cross when I see him,
the way he wrinkles up his short-sighted eyes is so
disarming.

He had absolutely no excuse except that he
had run across old friends, and they had persuaded
him to stay to lunch, and then they had got talking,
and so on and so on.   He was very repentant, but
inclined to laugh.   I expect really he had forgotten
for the time he had a sister.   He confessed he
hadn't mentioned my existence till he was leaving,
and then, he said, " They did seem rather surprised "
I should think so indeed !

Our home mail was waiting us at Manpur and
another " Calcutta " dinner.   Your letter, my

faithful friend, was more than usually charming
and kind—a balm to my lacerated feelings ! If
you don't get a letter next mail after this it will
mean either that we are entirely out of the reach
of post offices, or that a tiger has eaten the dâk-
runner.

Chota Haganpore, March 25.

. . . A WHOLE fortnight since I wrote last, and
our tour is almost over.   On Wednesday we go back
to Calcutta, and in April I sail for home.   The time
has simply rushed past.   This last fortnight has
been a time of pure delight ; I have been too ab-
sorbed in enjoying myself to write.

First, we stayed two days in a town where
Boggley had to open some sort of building.   The
natives met us with a band, and there were decora-
tions and mottoes and crowds.   In the evening a
dramatic entertainment took place for our amusement—*Julius Cæsar* acted by schoolboys.   Mark
Anthony wore a *dhoti*, a Norfolk jacket, and a bowler
hat.   In the middle of " Friends, Romans, Countrymen," the bowler fell off.   Still declaiming, he
picked it up with his toes, caught it with his hand,

and gravely put it on again—very much on one side. I envied the " mob " their serene calm of countenance. Boggley and I made horrible faces in our efforts to preserve our gravity.

The next day Boggley played in a football match with these same boys. One got a kick on the shin, and limping up to Boggley said, " Sir, I am wounded ; I cannot play," whereupon another ran up to the wounded one, crying, " Courage, brother. 'Tis a Nelson's death." Great dears I thought they were.

Since then we have been through dry places, and camped in desolate places, hardly ever seeing a European, and enjoying ourselves extremely. One day, a red-letter day, Boggley shot two crocodiles. One was a fish-eater, but the other was a great old *mugger*, most loathsome to look at. Autolycus hoped for *human limbs* inside it, and I believe they did actually find relics of his gruesome meals in the shape of anklets and rings and bangles. Boggley is going to have the skins made up into things for me, but it will take about six months to cure them. It is good to think there is one *mugger* the less. I hate the nasty treacherous beasts. Pretending they are logs, and then eating the poor natives !

One night we had a delightful camping-ground
on the edge of a lochan well stocked with duck
which Boggley set out to shoot and ended by missing
gloriously. We were much embarrassed by a fat
old landowner heaping presents on us He nearly
wept when we refused to accept a goat !

All the fortnight we have only met two Europeans
—a couple called Martin. I don't know quite what
they were, or why they were holding up the flag
of empire in this lonely outpost, but they were the
greyest people I ever saw.

Finding ourselves in the neighbourhood of
Europeans, we called, as in duty bound. The compound round the bungalow had a dreary look, and
when we were shown into the drawing-room I could
see at a glance it was a room that no one took any
interest in. The rugs on the floor were rumpled,
the cushions soiled ; photographs stood about in
broken frames, and the flowers were dying in their
glasses. When Mrs. Martin came in, I wasn't surprised at her room. A long grey face, lack-lustre
eyes, greyish hair rolled up anyhow, and greyish
clothes with a hiatus between the bodice and skirt.
" This," said I to myself, " is a woman who has lost
interest in herself and her surroundings." Her
husband was small and bleached-looking and,

given encouragement, inclined to be jokesome ;
sometimes (by accident) he was funny. Mrs.
Martin paid very little attention to us, and none
whatever to her husband's jokes. I laughed loudly
I thought it was so persevering of him to go on trying
to be funny when he was married to such a depressing
woman. As we got up to go I noticed in a corner
a child's chair with a little chintz cover, and seated
in it a smiling china doll lacking one arm and a leg.

I could hardly wait till I was outside to tell
Boggley what I thought of Mrs. Martin and her
house. " The hopeless, untidy creature ! " I raved
" She doesn't deserve to have such a little cheery
husband or children."

The only thing I don't like about Boggley is that
he never will help me to abuse people.

" Poor woman," he said ; " she's pretty bad "
Then he told me her story as he had heard it.

Ten years ago, it seems, she was quite a cheery
managing woman, with two little girls whom she
worshipped ; she and her husband lived for the
children. They were just going to take them home
when they sickened with some ailment. Mr
Martin at the time was prostrate after a bad attack
of fever. There was no doctor within thirty miles.
One child died, and the mother started with the

other on the long drive to the nearest doctor. The
last ten miles it was a dead child she held in her
arms.

When Boggley finished I was silent, remembering
the little chintz-covered chair—empty but for a
broken doll.

Now that I have tasted the joys of solitude I
don't see how I am to enjoy living in a crowd again.
I am practically alone all day, for Boggley has long
distances to ride and bicycle—and I never was so
happy in my life. I write, and I read, and I fold
my hands in newly acquired Oriental calm (which
my bustling, busy little mother most certainly
won't admire), and sit looking before me for hours.

The books lent me by various people are all read
long ago, and I have gone back to those that are
always with me.

They are all before me as I write. The little fat
green one at the end of the row is Lamb's *Essays of
Elia*. he so well fits some moods, and certain
minutes of the day, that gentle writer. Next is my
Pilgrim's Progress, the one I have had since my
tenth birthday. Father gave each of us a copy
when we reached the mature age of ten. It was
only on high days and holy-days that we were
allowed to look at his own treasured copy, which

stayed behind glass doors in the corner book-case
The illustrations, I know now, were very fine,
and even then we found them wonderful. Then
comes my little old Bible. I coveted it for years
before I got it because it had pages like five-pound
notes ; I value it now for other reasons. Next the
Bible is Q's *Anthology of English Verse*, its brave
leather cover rather impaired by the fact that for
two mornings Boggley, having mislaid his strop,
has stropped his razor on it. Lastly comes my
Shakespeare.

Sometimes in a night-marish moment I wonder
what the world would have been like had there
been no Shakespeare. Suppose we had never
known Falstaff, never heard the Clown sing " O
Mistress Mine," never laughed with Beatrice nor
masqueraded with Rosalind, never thrilled when
Cleopatra " again for Cydnos to meet Mark Antony "
cries " Give me my robe, put on my crown ; I
have immortal longings in me."

What would we do when surfeited with the
company of those around us if we couldn't creep
away and pass for a little while into the company
of those immortals ? What does it matter how
tiresome and complacent people are when I am
Orsino inviting the Clown to sing words the

utter beauty of which bring the tears to my
eyes .

> "O fellow, come, the song we had last night :
> Mark it, Cesario ; it is old and plain
> The spinsters and the knitters in the sun,
> And the free maids that weave their thread with bones,
> Do use to chant it ; it is silly sooth,
> And dallies with the innocence of love,
> Like the old age "

One never comes to the end of the beauty. Only
to-day, while I was browsing for a few minutes in
a comedy I have not much acquaintance with, I
happened on these lines, which I am going to write
down merely for the pleasure of writing them ·

"I am a woodland fellow, sir, that always loved
a great fire, and the master I speak of ever keeps
a good fire. I am for the house with the narrow
gate, which I take to be too little for pomp to enter .
some that humble themselves may, but the many
will be too chill and tender, and they'll be for the
flowery way that leads to the broad gate and the
great fire."

A very pleasant thing about our present solitude
is that one can read aloud or speak to oneself without
risk of being thought demented. The fact is, the
inhabitants of the little village on the outskirts
of which we are camping regard us as so hopelessly and utterly mad already that no further

display of eccentricity on our part could make any difference.

Even in the jungle there are servant troubles. Our cook, finding, I expect, this life too uneventful, intimated that his father was dying, and left last night We thought we should have to go without dinner, but Autolycus, stepping gallantly into the breach, said No, he would cook it; he had often cooked while with Colonel-M'Greegor-Sahib. The next we saw was a hen flying wildly, pursued by Autolycus, and in about half an hour it appeared on the table, its legs—still rather feathery—sticking protestingly from the dish. That was all there was for dinner except two breakfast-cups of muddy coffee.

. . . The dâk came in a little while ago with the English mail. I have just finished reading your letter. I think I know what you must feel about your book. It is sad to come to the end of a long and pleasant task—something finished you won't do again, a page of life closed. I know. It scares me, too, how quickly things come to an end. We are hurrying on so, the years pass so quickly, that even a long life is a terribly short darg. Life is such a happy thing. one would like it to last. I was twenty-six yesterday, and if my soul were to

14

say to me now, "*Finish, good lady, the bright day is over,*" I would be most dreadfully sorry (and I would expect everyone else to be dreadfully sorry too ; I'm afraid I would insist on a great moaning at the bar when I put out to sea) ; but I would have to admit that I have had a good time—a good, good time.

But I don't agree with you about the darkness of what comes after. How can it be dark when the Sun of Righteousness has arisen ? I suppose it must be very difficult for clever people to believe, the wise and prudent who demand a reason for everything ; but Christ said that in this the foolish things of the world would confound the wise. I am glad He said that. I am glad that sometimes the battle is to the weak. At the crossing, " I sink," cried Christian, the strong man, " I sink in deep waters," but Much-Afraid went through the river singing, though none could understand what she said. I don't know that I could give you a reason for the hope that is in me (I speak as one of the " foolish things "), but this I know, that if we hold fast to the substance of things hoped for, the evidence of things not seen, looking to Jesus, the author and finisher of our faith, then, when the end comes, we shall be able to lay our heads down like children saying, *This night when I lie down to sleep,* in the sure and certain hope that when, having done with houses made with hands, we wake up in the House of Many Mansions, it will be what John Bunyan calls a " sunshine morning."

I shall have to stop writing, though lecturing you is a fascinating pastime, for the day is almost done, and Boggley will soon be home.

Autolycus, looking very worried, is busied with the task of preparing the evening meal. One of the *chuprassis,* his gaudy uniform laid aside, and clad in a fragment of cotton, is sluicing himself with water and praying audibly. The *dhobi* is beating our clothes white on stones in the tank. In the village the women are grinding corn ; the oxen are drawing water from the well. The wood-smoke hangs in wisps on the hot air, and the song of the boys bringing home the cattle comes to me distinctly in the stillness. The sunset colours are fading into the deep blue of the Indian night, and the faithful are being called to prayer.

At home they are burning the whins on the hill-sides, and the Loch o' the Lowes lies steel-grey under the March sky.

THE LAND OF REGRETS

Calcutta, April 1 *(Monday).*

. . . The flesh-pots of Calcutta are wonderfully pleasant after jungly fare, and there is something rather nice about a big airy bedroom with a bathroom to correspond, hot water at will, and an *ayah* to look after one's clothes, after the cramped space of a tent, a zinc bath wiggling on an uneven floor, and Autolycus fumbling vaguely among one's belongings. I am staying with G. in her sister's, Mrs. Townley's, very charming house. Boggley had to go off at once on another short tour, and I was only too pleased to come to this most comfortable habitation. It is nice to be with G. again, and she has lots to tell me about her doings—dances, garden-parties, picnics—all of which she has enjoyed thoroughly. All the same, I would rather have had my jungle experiences. She and her sister and brother-in-law laugh greatly at my tales. They regard me as an immense joke, I don't know why. I think myself I am rather a sensible, serious sort of person.

Mrs. Townley is the kindest woman. She has

such a delightful way of making you feel that you are doing her the greatest favour by accepting her hospitality. I am not the only guest. A member of a nursing sisterhood—Sister Anna Margaret— is resting here for a few days. She wears clothes quite like a nun, but she is the cheeriest soul, with such contented eyes. She might be a girl, from the interest she takes in our doings and the way she laughs at our well-meant but not very witty fun.

Calcutta is very hot. The punkahs go all day —not the flapping kind of Mofussil punkahs, but things like bits of windmills fastened to poles. I never like to sit or sleep exactly underneath one, they look so insecure ; besides, they make one so untidy. At a dinner-party it is really dreadful to have the things flap-flapping above one's carefully done hair. My hair needs no encouragement to get untidy, and I have quite an Ophelia-like air before we get to the fish. It is too hot to go out much except very early in the morning and again after tea. We read and write and work till luncheon, then go to bed and try to sleep till tea-time. We waken hot and very cross, and it is the horridest thing to get up and get into a dress that seems to fasten with millions of hooks and buttons. My old

Bella is back with me, but she has found a mistress
whose temper has shortened as the temperature
has risen. Yesterday she fumbled so fastening my
dress that I jumped round on her, stamped my
foot, and said, " Bella, I shall slap you in a minute."
She replied in such a reproving tone, " Oh ! Missee
Baba." Tea makes one feel better, and then there
is tennis and a drive in the cool of the evening.

Mosquitoes are a great trial. They don't worry
so much through the day, but at night—at night,
when one with infinite care has examined the inside
of the mosquito-curtains to make sure none are
lurking, and then, satisfied, has dived into bed
and tucked the curtain carefully round, and is just
going off to sleep—buzz-z-z sounds the hateful
thing, and all hope of a quiet night is gone. The
other night I woke and found G. springing all over
her bed like a kangaroo. At first I thought she
had gone mad, dog-like, with the heat, but it
turned out she was only stalking a mosquito.

Yesterday we all went—Mrs. Townley, Sister
Anna Margaret, G., and I—to the Calcutta Zoo. We
fed the monkeys with buns, watched the loathly
little snakes crawl among the grass in their cages,
and then G. began gratuitously to insult a large
fierce tiger by poking at it with her sunshade.

It wasn't a kind thing to do, for it is surely bad enough to be caged without having a sunshade poked at one, and evidently the tiger thought so, for it lashed its tail and its roars shook the cage. We went home, and retribution followed swift and sure.

The first floor of the house consists of the drawing-room and two enormous bedrooms, one opening into the other, and both opening by several windows on to the verandah. Sister Anna Margaret is in one, G. and I in the other. We have two beds, but they are drawn close together and covered by a mosquito-curtain. Last night we went to bed in our usual gay spirits and fell asleep. It seemed to me that we were in the Zoo again and the tiger was fiercer than ever. It hit the bars with its great paw, and to my horror I saw that the bars were giving. I ran, but it was too late. The beast was out of the cage and coming after me with great bounds. My legs went round in circles and made no progress, as legs do in dreams; the tiger sprang— and I woke. At first I lay quiet, too thankful to find myself in bed to think about anything else; then I sniffed.

" Olivia ? " said G.   " Do you notice it ? "

" What ? " I asked.

" That awful smell of Zoo."

Of course that was it. I had been wondering what was the curious smell. My first thought—an awful one—was that the tiger had actually broken loose, tracked us home, and was now under the bed waiting to devour us. There was nothing to hinder it but a mosquito-curtain ! How I accomplished it, paralysed as I was with terror, I know not, but I took a flying leap and landed on G., hitting her nose with my head and clutching wildly at her brawny arms, much developed with tennis, as my only refuge.

She was too terrified to resent my intrusion.

" What do you think it is ? " she whispered. " Hu-s-h, speak low. Perhaps it doesn't know there's anyone in the room."

" It's the tiger from the Zoo," I hissed with conviction.

G. started visibly. " Rubbish," she said. " A tiger wouldn't get into a house. Ah—oh, listen ! "

Distinctly we heard the fud of four feet going round the bed.

" Cry for help," said G.

" Sister ! " we yelled together.

" Sister Anna ! "

" Sister Anna Margaret ! "

No answer. Sister Anna Margaret slept well.

" Sister ! " said G. bitterly. " She's no sister in adversity."

" Get up, G.," I said encouragingly. " Get up and turn on the light. Perhaps it isn't a tiger, perhaps it's only a musk rat."

G. refused with some curtness. " Get up yourself," she added.

Again we shouted for Sister, with no result.

You have no idea how horrible it was to lie there in the darkness and listen to movements made by we knew not what. We felt bitterly towards Sister Anna, never thinking of what her feelings would be if she came confidingly to our help and was confronted by some fearsome animal.

" If only," said G., " we knew what time it was and when it will be light. I can't *live* like this long. Let go my arm, can't you ? "

" I daren't," I said. " You're all I've got to hold on to."

We lay and listened, and we lay and listened, but the padding footsteps didn't come back ; and then I suppose we must have fallen asleep, for the next thing we knew was that the *ayahs* were standing beside us with tea, and the miserable night was past.

G. and I looked at each other rather shame-
facedly.

" Did we dream it ? " I asked

G. was rubbing her arm where I had gripped it.

" I didn't dream this, anyway," she said ; " it's
black and blue."

At breakfast we knew the bitterness of having
our word doubted ; no one believed our report.
They laughed at us and said we had dreamt it, or
that we had heard a mouse, and became so offensive
in their unbelief that G. and I rose from the table
in a dignified way, and went out to walk in the
compound.

We are very busy collecting things to take home
with us.   (Did I tell you G.'s berth had been booked
in the ship I sail in—the *Socotra*—it sails about the
23rd ?)   The *chicon-wallah* came this morning and
spread his wares on the verandah floor—white rugs
from Kashmir, embroidered gaily in red and green
and blue ; tinsel mats and table centres : pieces of
soft bright silk ; dainty white sewed work. We
could hardly be dragged from the absorbing sight
to the luncheon-table.

The Townleys never change their servants, and
now three generations serve together. The old
kitmutgar is the grandfather and trains his grand-

sons in the way which they should go. To-day at
luncheon (fortunately we were alone), one of them
made a mistake in handing a dish, whereupon his
grandfather gave him a resounding box on the
ears, knocking off his turban. Instead of going
out of the room, the boy went on handing me
pudding, sobbing loudly the while, and with tears
running down his face. It was very embarrassing,
and none of us had enough Hindustani to rebuke
the too-stern grandparent.

Later.

This afternoon, when we·were having tea in the
garden and enjoying Peliti's chocolate-cake, a great
outcry arose from the house, and we saw the servants
running and looking up to the verandah. Mr·
Townley called out to know what was the matter,
and received such a confused jumble of Hindustani
in reply that he went to investigate. He came back
shrugging his shoulders. " It's some nonsense
about a ' spirit.'   They say it's been appearing
suddenly, then disappearing for some time. Now
the *chokra* swears he saw it go up the verandah
into a bedroom. To satisfy them, I have sent for
my gun, and I'll wait below while they drive the
' spirit ' down."

" It's our midnight visitor," G. and I cried together.

We waited, breathless. The servants rushed
on to the verandah with sticks—a dark streak slid
down the verandah pillar—Mr. Townley fired. It
wasn't a tiger, it was a civet cat—a thing rather
like a fox, with a long pointed nose and an un-
commonly nasty smell.

" Think,"said G., as we looked at it lying stretched
out stiff,—" think of having that thing under our
bed !   A mouse indeed ! "

We didn't say " I told you so," but we looked it.

Boggley comes back to-morrow, and I am going
with him to the Grand Hotel, so that we shall be
together for the last little while.

Agra, April 11.

. . FROM a chapter in the *Arabian Nights* ; from
the middle of the most gorgeous fairy-tale the mind
of man could invent, I write to you to-night.

Often I have heard of the Taj Mahal, read of its
beauty, dreamed of its magic, but never in my
dreams did I imagine anything so exquisite, so
perfect.

Boggley thought I should not leave India without
seeing this " miracle of miracles—the final wonder
of the world," so we left Calcutta on Monday night
by the Punjab mail and came to Agra, and we have
done it all in proper order. Yesterday, in the
morning, we motored to the deserted city, the
capital of Akbar, the greatest of the Mogul em-
perors, about twenty miles off. It has battlemented
walls and great gates like a fairy-tale city. The
bazaar part of it is mostly in ruins, but the royal
part is perfectly preserved and could be lived in
comfortably now. There is Akbar's Council
Chamber, the houses of his wives, the courtyard
where they played living chess, the stables, water-
works, the palaces of his chief ministers, the mosque
and cloisters, the Gate of Victory. The carving in
marble and red sandstone is wonderful. Akbar
must have been a broad-minded man, for we found
paintings of the Annunciation side by side with
pictures of the Hindu god Ganesh. It is intensely
interesting to see the place just as it was hundreds
of years ago. In the great Mosque Quadrangle
there is a marble mausoleum, delicately carved, a
priceless piece of work in mother-of-pearl, erected
to Akbar's high priest ; and our guide was his lineal
descendant, glad to get five rupees for his trouble !

We lunched in the Government bungalow, a comfortable place, not glaringly out of keeping with the surroundings, and then motored to Akbar's tomb—another piece of colossal magnificence. I was awed by it. Out of the glaring sunshine we went down a long dark passage to a great vault, where the air was cold with the coldness of death. It was completely dark except for one ray of light falling on the plain marble tomb. An old Mohammedan crooned eerily, impressively, a lament which echoed round and round the vault. The Mohammedans and the Scots have a similar passion for deaths and funerals !

Lastly, in its fitting order, we drove to the Taj Mahal.

You know the story ? I have just been reading about it in Steevens's book. You know how Shah Jehan, grandson of Akbar, first Mogul Emperor of Hindustan, loved and married the beautiful Persian Arjmand Banu,—called Mumtaz-i-Mahal,—and when she died he, in his grief, swore that she should have the loveliest tomb the world ever beheld, and for seventeen years he built the Taj Mahal ? You know how after thirty years his son rose up and dethroned him, and kept him a close prisoner for seven years in the Gem Mosque, where his daughter

15

Jehanara attended him and would not leave him.
When grown very feeble he begged to be laid where
he could see the Taj Mahal ; and, the request being
granted, you know how he died with his face towards the tomb of the beautiful Persian, " whose
palankeen followed all his campaigns in the days
when Empire was still a-winning, whose children
called him father—Arjmand Banu, silent and un-
seen now for four-and-thirty years, the wife of his
youth "

Such a passionate old story ! Such a marvellous
love-memorial ! Shah Jehan—Mumtaz-i-Mahal—
Grape Garden—Golden Pavilion—Jasmine Tower·
As G. W. Steevens says, there is dizzy magic in the
very names. I am no more capable of describing
it than I would have been capable of building it ;
you must see it for yourself. It alone is worth
coming to India to see.

Leaving the Taj Mahal dazed and dizzy with
beauty, I was hailed by a voice that sounded
familiar, and turning round I saw—an incongruous
figure in that Arabian Nights garden — our old
friend of the *Scotia*, the Rocking Horse Fly. She
had another female with her, and Mr. Brand, the
funny man who asked conundrums. I'm afraid
my eyes had asked what he was doing in this galley,

or he hastily said that he had only arrived in Agra
hat morning, and found our *Scotia* acquaintance
it the hotel. I introduced Boggley, and we stood
incomfortably about, while the Rocking Horse Fly
vaxed sentimental over our meeting.

" Isn't it odd," she said, " that we should all meet
ind just part again ? "

I thought it would have been much odder (and
iow infinitely horrible !) if we had all met and never
)arted. As it happened, we weren't allowed to part
vith her as soon as we could have wished. She dis-
:overed we were staying at the same hotel, so we
iad to dine together, and she talked the Taj all
.hrough dinner, spattering it with adjectives, while
Boggley grunted at intervals. It was refreshing to
.ee Mr. Brand again He seems to be enjoying
india vastly, and had three quite new stories, though
f he didn't laugh so much telling them it would be
:asier to see the point. Boggley and he loved each
)ther at once. After dinner, when the men were
:moking, the Rocking Horse Fly began to get arch
—don't you hate people when they are arch ?—and
:aid surely I was never going home without cap-
:uring some heart. I replied stoutly and truthfully
:hat I was.

" Naughty girl ! " said the R.H.F. " You

haven't made the most of your opportunities. Don't you know what they call girls who come out for the cold weather ? "

I said I didn't.

" They are called ' The Fishing Fleet,' " she said sweetly

I said " Oh," because I didn't know what else to say, feeling as I did so remiss.

I have heard—Mr. Townley told me—that long ago when a ship from England arrived in the Hoogly a cannon was fired, and all the gay bachelors left their offices and went to the docks to appraise the new arrivals. A ball was given on board on the night of arrival, and many of the girls were engaged before they left the ship. I don't object to that. It was a fine, sincere way of doing things ; but why the subject of marriage should be made an occasion for archness, for sly looks, for—in extreme cases— nudgings, passes my comprehension.

The R.H.F. has a way of making common any subject she touches—even the Taj and marriage— so I thought I would go to bed. As I said good-night I regarded attentively the friend, wondering much how anyone could, of choice, accompany the R.H.F. in her journeyings. She is a very silent person, large and fat and about forty, and her eyes are small

out of all proportion to her face, but they twinkled
at me in such an understanding way that I, generally
so chary of offering embraces, went up to kiss her.
She is kind, but so large that being kissed by her is
almost as destroying as being in a railway accident!

Do I ignore what you say in your letter? You
see, it is rather difficult. Writing to a friend in a
far country is like shouting through a speaking-tube
to the moon, and one can't shout very intimate
things, can one?

Let us be sensible. Don't be angry, but are you
quite sure you really care, and is it wise to care?
We are so very different. You are so very English,
and I, in spite of a pink and fluffy exterior, am at
heart as bitter and dour and prejudiced as any
Covenanter that ever whined a psalm. My mind
could never have anything but a Scots accent. You
are reserved and rather cold, I am expansive to
a fault. You are terrifyingly clever; my intelli-
gence is of the feeblest. You have a refined sense
of humour; the poorest, most obvious joke is good
enough for me   But this is only talk. I don't
know that I am " in love,"—I don't like the expression anyway.—but this I know, that if you were not
in the world it would be an unpeopled waste to me.
The place you happen to be in is where all interest

centres. Every minute of the time as I go through
my days, laughing, talking, enjoying myself vastly,
away at the back of my mind the thought of you
lies "hidden yet bright," making for me a new
heaven and a new earth. Is this caring? Is this
what you want to hear me say? I can't write what
I would like, I can't weave pretty things, I can
only speak straight on, but oh, my dear, I am so
glad that in this big, confusing world we have found
each other. Poor Rocking Horse Fly! poor fat
friend! how dull for them, how dull for all the rest
of the people in the world not to have a you!

I am not going to write any more, not because I
haven't lots to say, but because writing much or
talking much about a thing—being queer and Scots,
it is hard for me to say love—seems somehow to
cheapen it, profane it.

   .   .   .   .   .   .

I have opened this just to say again, My dear,
my dear!

                           Calcutta, April 21.

. . . ONLY three more days in India, and I don't
know whether I am horribly sorry to go or pro-

foundly relieved to get away.   There is no doubt it
is a sudden and dangerous country.   Three people
we knew have died suddenly of cholera, and two
others have had bombs thrown at them.   I shall
be thankful to find myself safely on board the
steamer, but even if I escape I am leaving Boggley
in the midst of these perils.   Not that he lets the
thought of them vex his soul.   You learn, he says,
to look upon death in a different way in India, but
I am sure I never could learn to regard with equan-
imity the thought of being quite well one day and
being hurried away to the Circular Road Cemetery
early the next.   It is sad to die in a foreign land,
and it is somehow specially sad, at least I think so,
for a home-loving Scot to lie away from home.

> " Tell me not the good and wise
> Care not where their dust reposes,
> That to him who sleeping lies
> Desert rocks shall seem as roses.
> I've been happy above ground,
> I could ne'er be happy under,
> Out of Teviot's gentle sound
> Part us, then, not far asunder."

Yesterday I saw a pathetic sight.   A couple in
a *tikka-gharry* ; the man a soldier, a Gordon High-
lander, and on the front seat a tiny coffin.   The
man's arm was round the woman's shoulder, and
she was crying bitterly.   A bit of shabby crape

was tied round her hat, and she carried a sad little wreath.

Since coming back from Agra we have stayed at the Grand Hotel   It is a comfortable, airy place, wonderfully pleasant in the morning when we sit at a little table in the verandah looking out on the Maidan, and flat-faced hill-waiters bring us an excellent breakfast   Our own servants are with us—Autolycus and Bella.   When we arrived very early in the morning and the coolies were carrying up our luggage, a servant sleeping outside his master's door held up his hand for quietness, say· ing something quite gently about not waking his master.   "Beat him," said Autolycus to the coolies quite without heat, as he hurried on.

The air gets hotter, and everything looks more and more tired every day.   Even proud-pied April dressed in all its trim can't put a spirit of youth into anything.

But these last days in Calcutta, in spite of fears and heat, are very pleasant   I don't know how I could have said the Calcutta women were horrid ! Now that I am going to leave them they seem so kind and attractive   Every minute of my time is filled up .with river-picnics, garden-parties, tennis tournaments, dinners and theatre parties ; and

my mornings are spent with G. raking in queer
shops for curiosities. I am insatiable for
things to take home, and Autolycus has packed
and roped three large wooden boxes containing my
treasures.

I wish life weren't such a mixed thing. Just
when I am tiptoeing on the heights of joy because
I am going home, I am brought to common earth
with a thud by the miserable thought that I must
leave Boggley. (How pleasant it would be to have
a sort of spiritual whipping-boy to bear the nasty
things in life for one—the disappointments, the
worries, the times of illness and sorrow, the partings)
Boggley says it will be all right once I am away.
As a rule he only feels pleasantly home-sick. Now,
with the preparations for departure constantly
before him, helping to address boxes to the familiar
old places, going with me in imagination from port
to port till we reach cool Western lands, I'm afraid
he has many a pang.

I am so sorry you are so worried. You will
almost have got my letter by this time, but I wish
I had cabled as you asked, only, somehow, I didn't
like the idea. I thought you knew I cared; but,
after all, how could you ? I didn't know myself
when I left England. Looking back I seem always

to have cared immensely. How could I help it ?
What I can't understand is how every woman of
your acquaintance doesn't care as I do ; you seem
to me so lovable. I am so glad (though it seems an
odd thing to be glad about !) that you have no
mother and no sister. I don't feel such a marauder
as I would have done if, by taking you, I had
robbed some other woman   And I am glad of your
lonely life. I shall be able to show you what a nice
thing a home is. A quiet, safe place we shall make
it, where worldly cares may not enter. Boggley
says I can make an hotel room look home-like, and,
indeed, it is almost my only accomplishment, this
talent for home-making. There is one thing I want
to say to you. You know what Robert Louis says
about married men ?—that there is no wandering
in pleasant bypaths for them, that the road lies
long and straight and dusty to the grave. It dulls
me to think of it. *Don't* feel that. Don't let it
be true. We mustn't let our lives get dusty and
straight and narrow. We shall love whimsies and
we shall laugh. So long as laughter isn't heartless
and doesn't hurt anyone it is good to laugh. Life
will see to it that there are tears—at least I'm
told so. But suppose in years to come, after we
have grown used to each other (though it does

amaze me that people should talk about things
losing their charm because one gets *used* to them.
Does a child tire of its mother because it is used
to her? Is Spring any the less wonderful because
we are used to her coming? God grant we have
many years to get used to each other !)—suppose
one fine morning you find that life has lost its
savour, you are tired of the accustomed round, you
are tired of the house, you are tired of the look of
the furniture, you want to get away for a time—
in a word, to be free. Well, remember, you are
not to feel that the road isn't clear before you. I
promise you not to feel aggrieved. I shan't wonder
how my infinite variety could have palled. I
know that all men—men who are men—at times
hear the Red Gods call them (women hear them
too, you know, only they have more self-control ;
they find their peace in fearful innocence and household laws), and I shall be waiting on the doorstep
when you return from climbing Kangchenjunga,
or exploring the Bramahputra Gorges, ready to
say, " Come away in, for I'm sure you must be
tired."

Arthur, dear, am I a disappointing person, do
you find? Ought I to be able to write you different
sorts of letters, tenderer, more loving letters ?

But, you see, it wouldn't be me if I could. My
heart may be, indeed, I think it is, full of the
warmest instincts, but they have been unwinged
from birth so they can't fly to you. One of the
most talkative people living, in some ways I am
strangely speechless. Why! I haven't even told
Boggley, though if he had eyes to see instead of
being the blindest of dear old bats, my shining face
would betray me. I keep on smiling in a perfectly
imbecile manner, so that people exclaim, " Well,
you are indecently glad to get away," and when
they ask Why? I point them to the scene in the
Old Testament where Hadad said unto Pharaoh,
" *Let me depart, that I may go to mine own country.*"
*Then Pharaoh said unto him, " But what hast thou
lacked with me, that, behold, thou seekest to go to
thine own country?" And he answered, " Nothing :
howbeit let me go in any wise.*" So it is with me.
India has given me the best of good times. I have
lacked for nothing—" howbeit let me go in any
wise." You needn't think I am changed. I'm
not. I'm afraid I'm not. One would think that
a new environment would make a difference, but it
really does not. A person with a suburban mind
would be as suburban in the wilds of Nepal as in
the wilds of Tooting. The illuminating thought

has come to me that it isn't a man's environment
that matters, it's his mind. Haven't you often
noticed in an evening in London all the City men
hurrying home like rabbits to their burrows (not
the prosperous City men, but the lesser ones, whose
frock-coats are rather shiny and their silk hats
rather dull), and haven't you often thought how
narrow their lives are, how cramping their environment? But suppose one of those clerks loves
books and is something of a poet What does it
matter to him though his rooms in Clapham or
Brixton are grimy, almost squalid, and filled with
the worst kind of Victorian furniture? " Minds
innocent and quiet take such for an hermitage."
Once inside, the long day at the office over, and
the door shut on the world, an arm-chair drawn up
to the fire and his books around him he is as happy
as a king, for his mind to him is a Kingdom He
may be a puny little man, in bodily presence con-
temptible, but he will feel no physical disabilities
as he clambers on the wall of Jerusalem with
Count Raymond, or thrills as he sets forth with
Drake to fight Spaniards one against ten. Instead
of the raucous cries of the milk or the coal man,
he hears the horns of Elfland faintly blowing, and
instead of a window which can show him nothing

but a sodden plot planted with wearied-looking
shrubs, he has the key of that magic casement
which opens on perilous seas in fairylands forlorn.
He will never do anything great in the world, he
will never lead a forlorn hope, or marry the Princess,
or see far lands; he will never be anything but a
poor, shabby clerk, but he is of such stuff as
dreams are made of, and God has given to him
His fairyland.

No, I don't think a new environment changes
people, and it is foolish to think it makes them
forget. Sometimes in the Eden Gardens at sunset,
when we draw up to listen to the band, I watch
the faces of the youths—Scots boys come out from
Glasgow and Dundee—dreaming there in the Indian
twilight while the pipers play the tunes familiar to
them since childhood. They are sahibs out here,
they have a horse to ride and a servant to look
after them, things they never would have had had
they stayed in Dundee or Glasgow, but though
they are proud they are lonely. What does grandeur
matter if " the Quothquan folk " can't see it?
The peepul trees rustle softly overhead, the languor-
ous soft air laps them round, the scent of the East
is in their nostrils, but their eyes are with their
hearts, and is this what they see? A night of

drizzling rain, a street of tall, dingy, grey houses,
and a boy, his day's work done, bounding upstairs
three steps at a time to a cosy kitchen where the
tea is spread, where work-roughened hands at his
coming lift the brown teapot from the hob, and a
kind mother's voice welcomes him home at the
end of the day. . . .

Autolycus has knocked at the door to say
" Master's come " (he likes to be very European
with me so doesn't call him Sahib), and I must go
to tea. To-morrow Boggley is taking the whole
day off and we have got it all planned out, every
minute of it. In the morning we shall drive in a
tikka-gharry to the Stores to buy some final
necessaries (such as soap and tooth-powder), then
to Peliti's to eat ices, then to the shop in Park
Street so that Boggley may get me a delayed birthday present, then round and round the Maidan.
Then we shall go to luncheon at the Townleys and
go on with them to Tollygunge for golf. *Then* we
are going to tea with some people who are taking
us a motor run. *Then* we go to a farewell dinner
at the Ormondes'. Then we shall go to bed.

Bless you, my dear.

S.S. Socotra, Homeward Bound,
Somewhere in the Hoogly, April 24.

. . . THIS day seems to have been going on for
weeks and it is only tea-time now. Was it only
this morning that we left ? I can't think it was
this morning that Boggley and I took our last
chota-hazri together, and Boggley as he gloomily
sugared his tea, said, " Now I know what a con-
demned man feels like on the morning of his execution." Then we laughed and it wasn't so bad.
Autolycus, very important because the Miss Sahib
was going to cross the Black Water, bustled about
with my few packages (all the heavy baggage went
away two days ago) and, finally, bustled us into a
tikka-gharry in such good time that we had to drive
twice round the Maidan before we went to the
landing-stage. Dear, funny Autolycus ! I shall
miss his ugly, honest face. He has added greatly
to the gaiety of nations as represented by Boggley
and me. The last we saw of him was standing
before the hotel door along with Bella and the two
chuprassis bowing low and murmuring, " Salaam,
Miss Sahib, salaam," while I, undignified to the
last, knelt on the seat and wildly waved a handker-
chief

The landing was crowded with people. I wondered how we were all to get on board one ship, but found as we got on to the launch that most of the people remained behind; they were only see-ers off. Mr. Townley had by some means managed to get permission for himself, his wife, and Boggley to go down the river with us in the launch to where the *Socotra* lay; which was a great comfort to us all. When we found our party, poor G.'s face was much less pink than usual. The Ormondes were there, having ridden down to see us off, and quite a lot of other people had come for the same reason. We (the passengers) had to be medically examined before we were allowed to leave—in case of plague, I suppose. G. and I were rather scared at the thought—how were we to know that we hadn't plague lurking about us? However, after a very cursory glance we were passed on, got our good-byes said, and embarked on the launch. At any other time I would have hated saying good-bye to the Ormondes and the other dear peoople, but with the parting from Boggley looming so near, I was absent-minded and callous, though I hope I didn't appear so. The *Socotra* is quite a tiny ship compared to the *Scotia*. G. and I clambered on board, in great haste to find

16

our cabin   We found it already occupied by our
cabin companion (she is Scotch and has artificial
teeth and a fine, rich Glasgow accent, and (I think)
is of a gentle and yielding disposition) and an enormous hat-box.

Boggley was with us, but when he saw we were
going to be firm he fled.

" This," said G., waving her hand towards
the offending box, " must go into the baggage-
room."

" Certainly," said the Glasgow woman. " I'm
sure I don't know what it's doing here.   Ma husband
wrote the labels." And she actually began to
drag it into the passage.

Seeing her so amenable to reason, we smiled
kindly and begged her to desist.   But she said,
" Not at all," and smiled back in such a delightfully Glasgow " weel-pleased " way that my heart
warmed to her.   I can see she will be a constant
entertainment.

Mr. Townley introduced us to the captain, who
looks kind, and who asked us to sit at his table,
and then we all went in to breakfast.   In spite
of our low spirits we enjoyed the meal.   G. created
something of a fracas about a kidney which she ate
and then said was bad, but she calmed down, and

we enjoyed looking at the other passengers, specu-
lating as to who and what they were.

Almost directly after breakfast our people had
to go, and G. and I, very stricken, watched the
launch as it steamed up the river till lost to sight
behind a big vessel. Since then, except for an
interval in the cabin to get our eyes bathed into
decency, we have sat on deck with aching heads,
trying to read and write. At first the heat was
terrible. We drooped like candles in the sun, we
wilted like flowers, and G. gasped, " If all the
voyage is going to be as hot as this, I'm done."
Limp and wretched, I agreed with her. Then we
found we had put our chairs against the kitchen,
which is up on deck in this ship.

No wonder we were warm ! We quickly found
a cooler spot, and I have been writing a long letter
to Boggley to send off with the pilot. Isn't he pure
gold, my Boggley ? I know that you too ' think
nobly of the soul." He will be home in a year,
and I am trying to tell myself that a year isn't
long. Well, the Indian trip is over, and I have
seen a lot, learned a few things, and made some
friends—best of them my faithful G. It is rather
astonishing that I should have the joy of her company home again. Many people, I am sure, ex-

pected she would remain in India, but I think she took the precaution to leave her heart at home, wise G. One thing you should be thankful for, there will be no more letters. What a blessing people are nicer than their letters ! How good you have been about mine, how willing to take an interest in the people I met, in the places I saw, in everything I told you about ; and when I was jocose, you pretended to be amused. Ah, well ! Be cheerful, sir, our revels now are ended !

And so I am going home, home to my own bleak kindly land, " place of all weathers that end in rain." I am going home to my own people (I think I see Peter jigging up and down in expectation before my trunks) ; and I am going to you. And the queer thing is, I can't feel glad. I am so home-sick for India. All my horror of bombs and sudden death has gone, and memory (as someone says) is making magic carpets under my feet, so that I am back again in the white, hot sunlight, under the dusty palm-trees, hearing the creak of the wagons, as the patient oxen toil on the long straight roads, and the songs of the coolies returning home at even. I see the country lying vague in the clammy morning mist, and the great broad Ganges glimmering wanly ; and again it is a wonderful clear night of stars I know that my own land is the best land, that the fat babu with his carefully oiled and parted hair and his too-apparent sock-suspenders can't be mentioned in the same breath as the Britisher; that our daffodils and primroses are sweeter far than the heavy-scented blossoms of the East; that the " brain-fever " bird of India is a wretched substitute for the lark and the thrush and others of " God's jocund little fowls "; that Abana and Pharpar and other rivers of Damascus are better than this Jordan—all this, I say, I know; but tonight I don't believe it.

India has thrown golden dust in my eyes, and I am seeing things all wrong. We have anchored for the night. . . . I am watching the misty green blur, which is all that is left to me of India, grow more and more indistinct as darkness falls. Soon it will be night.

G., who has been absolutely silent for more than an hour, sat up suddenly just now, and took my hand.

" Olivia," she said.   " It's a nice place, England." Her tone was the tone of one seeking reassurance.

" It is," I said dolefully.   " *Very.*"

" And it really doesn't rain such a great deal."

" No."

" Anyway, it's home, and India isn't, though India *has* been jolly." She sighed.

Then, " I shall enjoy a slice of good roast beef," said G.

Lightning Source UK Ltd.
Milton Keynes UK
08 December 2009

147248UK00001B/57/P